# A DRIFTING SUN

## EXILES: VOLUME ONE

### ASHLEY CAPES

*A Drifting Sun*
*(Exiles: 1)*
Copyright © 2023 by Ashley Capes

Cover: Illustration & Design by Vivid Covers
Layout & Typeset: David Schembri Studios




ISBN-978-0-6486237-0-0

www.ashleycapes.com

Published by Close-Up Books
Melbourne, Australia

*For the Backers!*

# CONTENTS

## PROLOGUE – THORN

The anniversary of a lie was seldom observed.

Yet Thorn recalled it no matter where he was at the time – be it a ravine of shifting darkness, a forest filled with whispers, a too-quiet inn – or, as now, in a marble-clad room while he waited for the tailor to finish measuring his shoulders. A new coat that might sparkle enough to catch the eye, but which would tell nothing of who wore it. *Not that I need such things.*

People saw only what Thorn wanted them to see.

All his lies in the kingdom of Nasaru were merely reiterations of the original lie. That he was, in fact, the king as everyone believed. But for fifteen years, his replacement of King Mutolo had gone unnoticed. *Not that they could penetrate my illusion, even if they tried.*

From such a lie, his long-held dream would finally come to pass…

"Your Majesty, I must apologise but I require more thread," the squat tailor said. "I will return with all swiftness."

Thorn nodded. "Take as much time as you need."

The tailor bowed and strode from the room, his footfalls suggesting no leisurely stroll. Thorn reached for his silk tunic where it had been slung over a chair, but a sweet tinkling of a bell stopped him.

Instead, he moved to the door and locked it. Turning back to the bell, it chimed again from where it rested beside a bookshelf lined with old tomes and animal figurines of stone.

The hidden door slid open, revealing Ibila, bearing a smile that was impossible not to return. She carried a leather satchel – no doubt filled with more yet-to-be-signed orders to provide funds to healers or food kitchens. Her red robe was sheer from halfway down her thighs, in an almost Senoja-military fashion, a golden necklace at her throat.

"If only they knew how hard the Young Fox of Omaila worked for others," he said.

She joined him, pressing the satchel into his hands. "No. Instead, they call me whore and assume I do nothing but pleasure you, Your Majesty." She paused. "And you know I don't care for that name; I am not young, nor am I an animal."

"Ibila is beautiful enough."

"Well, it's a real name, if nothing else." She draped her slender arms around his neck. "You are leaving soon, aren't you?"

"The demands of the court are varied and many."

"No, I meant for whatever it is that keeps you away for weeks at a time."

He nodded as he set the satchel down. "Will you place something into motion for me? I trust no-one else for this."

Ibila leant in to kiss him, a light touching of their lips only. "I must be easy to manipulate, since I enjoyed hearing that."

"Then you agree?"

"Tell me, and I will decide."

Gently, he unwrapped Ibila's arms and gestured for her to sit beside him upon the edge of the bed, the dark sheets soft. "There is an inevitable change due to fall upon the palace and the nation."

"You mean succession?"

"And after. Will my children squabble, will they tear apart what must be held together?"

"You have already told me you see no future upon a throne for half of your children. Ebatru excels in his role at the border, and you have even exiled your youngest boy already. Kiteka seems dedicated enough, but she is not the eldest – is it not then quite simple, according to tradition?"

"According to tradition, but I am no slave to the whims of my ancestors."

"What are you asking me to arrange, Mutolo?"

"Two things. Whatever you feel necessary to prepare for a dip into the world of your past life…"

She was frowning now.

"… and to watch those who might seek to block the final stage of construction for the Tree of Coral while I am gone. I believe they might have one last card to play. Especially Onga."

"I thought you were concerned about Duke Bedoa?"

"That matter is being dealt with."

"This statue *is* more than vanity, isn't it?" Ibila's tone revealed some concern, and a touch of accusation.

While it might not have been the kind of tone a king might accept from a mistress, Thorn was no king. "Of course."

"If you are asking me to sharpen my blades, then I would know why."

"That may not be likely – at least not for now," he said, taking her hands and giving them a gentle squeeze. "I am sending Kiteka to continue investigating the rebels, but like the Greyshields, I need her to find Asaro."

"And?"

"And if she attempts to use him for her own ends, then I would have her suffer a fatal accident."

Ibila sighed. "Then why send her to begin with?"

"Because she is capable where others may still fail."

"And Onga?"

"Whatever Onga is planning, I wish to know. He will make his moves, encouraged by knowledge that you will leak; I am to leave the city."

"Very well."

"Alert General Tahbe to whatever you learn. Let him deal with our noble friend if it seems I will not return in time to act."

"Hmmm… Then you will finally tell me what the statue is for?"

Thorn found himself hesitating for the first time in a long time. What harm could come of telling Ibila? *A better question might be, can I trust anyone else?* The cost of being a liar, or lying for such a long time, was that any pool of true allies tended to shrink. "It will be a lure, for want of a clearer description. Strong enough to harness the power of the entire reef or beyond, should it be required."

"Are you exaggerating?"

"Not at all. You have seen how many sorcerers I have at work, hand in hand with the masons and sculptors."

"Of course."

"Once it is complete, the nation's future will be secured,

even after my time."

"I will do as you wish," she said, but there seemed more left upon her tongue. The flow of her thoughts was difficult to read, unlike those of most others in the palace, or anywhere, for that matter.

Instead, she raised his hand and pressed her lips against his palm.

## CHAPTER 1. – MEI

Iggy was gone.

Iggy was gone and Mei was pacing, even though she'd paused on the mountain trail to catch her breath. Her little brother's visit with their mother hadn't gone well – no visit ever did. Mei knew it, and not because she could read Iggy's expressions better than anyone else in the village. No, it wasn't like that at all.

He'd been born without a face; no-one could read him that way.

But the ground had rumbled during this morning's visit, putting everyone on edge before the earth settled once more.

Memories of Iggy's last psychic outburst still haunted the villagers. It had taken two weeks to clear the avalanche of stone that tumbled from the nearby Dalma Mountains and dammed the River Inrik. The collected telekinesis of those who called Nokema home had been their only saving grace.

Mei stopped her pacing to sit upon a warm slab of stone and take a few deep breaths. She waved away a pair of gleaming blue dragonflies as they darted by her head. *Slow down, idiot –*

*you won't catch him sprinting uphill.* The trail was steep enough to leave both calves aching, especially after a long morning spent foraging for the kema leaf.

*Get some sun.* She turned her palms up where they rested on her knees, tilting her chin too, and let the sunlight warm her face. And more. The rays energised her limbs too, sinking into her skin and muscles and, in time, her bones. "Ah."

Mei hopped down and resumed her climb.

Iggy's hut was almost an hour east of the village. A marvel he'd gotten so far ahead; her brother wasn't the most athletic of young men. Perhaps it was his fury. Would he still be angry? Still a danger to those around him?

But it wasn't Iggy's fault. Not really.

A sudden breeze picked up, blowing blonde tendrils of sweat-dampened hair into her eyes. Evening was falling, and it would soon grow cold. Best to spend the night in Iggy's hut and care for him, as she'd done many times before.

Since birth, and even before their mother sent him away, dreams he could not explain had plagued Iggy. Or maybe, dreams he *would* not explain. Mei never knew. Once, only once, he mentioned the moon, but that was all. She would soothe him back to sleep and then Iggy would be fine for the rest of the night, though he always refused to speak of the nightmares afterwards.

The villagers sniggered behind his back. They either believed he couldn't hear or they just didn't care. Most thought he was too old to seek her out after bad dreams too. But Ig chose her. Mei frowned. Each and every one of the villagers be damned; they had no idea what it was like–

The shrill cry of a falcon broke her reverie.

An empty trail ahead, no sign of the bird. Nothing but the dark green and blue of Olwor trees where they arched over hard earth. But the sound had been close. And its cry had carried a note of pain. Above, the sky was clear, with mere scuffs of cloud hovering around dark peaks of the Dalma.

At another call, she surged forward, tearing around a bend in the path. The bird was in pain. *Not again. Iggy.* "Please, let it be something natural," she breathed as she ran.

But lying in a patch of wildflowers beside the trail was a golden-brown falcon, its body twisted into a mess of blood and sticky feathers. Oddly, the grey of the curved beak was free of blood.

A young man crouched over the bird, his back to the trail. Frayed edges of his black cloak fluttered in the wind and his slender body was wracked by sobs. The breeze tugged at dark hair but his head did not turn at her approach.

"Iggy," she called.

His voice rang in her mind. *It was an accident, Mei. Again.* A clenched fist trembled at his side. *I* still *can't control it! Why?*

Mei exhaled as she halted behind him. "I know, Iggy."

*I'm older now. Why is it still happening?*

She rested a hand on his back, his trembling easing. "Want me to perform the ceremony?"

He shook his head. *No. But we should leave it to the insects, anyway.*

"I came to ask if you were all right... after... earlier," she finished, aware of the awkward pause.

*I'm fine.*

"Are you?" She started to kneel beside him, but he shrugged her off and leapt to his feet, running again, climbing as fast as he could without looking back.

*I don't want to talk about it, Mei.*

She hesitated. Iggy probably needed time but she wasn't going to give him too much. She'd follow soon enough to be sure.

But first...

She took out a stub of chalk and cleared the grass and flowers enough to leave a hard opening of stony earth. She drew a rough circle with the pale chalk, not making much of an impression, but it was better than nothing. She added rays to the circle, a poor rendition of the sun. "The sun find you," she murmured.

Then she rose and started after her brother.

***

Iggy's hut rested within a stand of pine and Olwor trees at the end of a winding trail.

The roof lay covered in dry needles and the incredibly hard, tear-shaped seeds of the Olwor. Behind her brother's home, the River Inrik ran back toward the village, sliding between trees at the bottom of a gentle slope. It murmured over rocks – no raging torrent here.

Mud and thatching patched gaps in the logs and a hinge on the door was in need of repair again. This far from Nokema, with nothing but the mouth of the river and the barren walls of the mountains to the east, few people travelled the road or the trail.

*Only me and Ig.*

Mei approached the hut slowly. It was almost dark beneath the trees and she shivered. Leaving the sun behind always hurt a little, for just a moment.

She knocked on the rough grain. "Iggy, it's me."

He didn't answer, but she knew he wouldn't. She pushed the door open and found him sitting in the window's fading light, head in his hands. The room was tidy, as ever. Fresh flowers stood in a vase he'd made himself and the fire pot was stacked with kindling, though the fireplace had not been lit. "I know what you're thinking."

*No, you don't. Not this time.*

He looked up finally and Mei studied him, watching for the slight signs of a psychic outburst. They could be hard to spot without facial cues to read. Only a smooth covering of skin and slight indentations marked his features. But the air did not grow still, nor did his hair take on a faint, golden tint.

*But I know what* you're *thinking, sister.*

"I'm sorry." It was an empty thing to say, but she couldn't help it. Her wariness was probably like flinching away from him... the way others did. "I don't mean to... I trust you, you know that."

He shrugged. *I don't blame you for hesitating; I would too.*

Mei stepped forward, reaching out to take his hands, smiling. They were slender, and though by no means strong, they could carve wondrous shapes. The bear on his windowsill, the apple in a bowl on his table and countless others, all were as lifelike as she'd ever seen – better than anything Nasaru merchants had ever brought to the village. How many times had she tried to convince Ig to sell them? The traders would take his carvings, but Iggy was too shy.

Mei drew a carving from one of the pouches on her belt. "I brought this back, Iggy... I thought you'd want it." She placed the object in his hands.

Iggy's head dipped as he ran a hand over the hard edges of quartz. Even without sight, Mei knew he saw the figurine he'd made for their mother. Iggy's vision came from his towering power – so great in fact, that the Paragons had once claimed Iggy had no face because he needed none.

A cruel thing to say.

"It looks just like him," Mei whispered.

*I thought she might have forgiven me by now.*

Mei didn't answer. Instead, she squeezed his hand and tried to lighten the mood. "Honestly, Ig. If your carving spoke, I'd swear it was a tiny version of Father."

*I miss him.*

"I know. I do too, especially in the spring."

*I'm sorry about the bird, Mei. After what Mother said today, I just got so angry. I wasn't meaning to–*

"I know." She put her arms around his thin shoulders.

*Why did she say that?*

Mei controlled her voice with some difficulty. "She shouldn't have said it. But she's hurting."

*So why does she have to hurt me too?*

"I know." Mei took the figurine from his hand and set it on the table. It really was a brilliant likeness of their father, a man that young Iggy had hardly known. Having no words to help her brother, Mei led him to the next room and helped him onto the bed. "You should rest."

Taking up a seat, she began to hum a wordless lullaby.

After a few moments of his silent weeping, Mei watched him drift off to sleep, the tension flowing from his limbs.

Only then did she let a tear of her own escape.

## CHAPTER 2. – MEI

Mei woke to a head full of sand and eyes thick with gunk. Light lanced through the window of the hut and she stretched slowly, pushing the blankets aside with clumsy hands. She'd slept well into morning – it had been a long night.

Iggy's nightmares were always bad after he visited their mother, but last night's one robbed her of true rest. As usual, he refused to talk about it. More so when she had noticed the bruises on his arms and forehead. Surrounded by darkness but for a slim box of moonlight on the floor, she flinched when she saw him. "You've hurt yourself again; let me help." She reached out to touch his head, but he caught her hand in both of his.

*I'm fine, Mei. Can you sing it again?*

"Of course." She examined the bruises, which weren't too bad. "But you can tell me, you know," Mei had said, before humming the lullaby once more.

Now she stood within the patch of light for a moment before poking her head into his bedroom. The cot was empty. From outside, she heard light footsteps and birdsong, an innocent-seeming cheer.

She pulled her pants on then laced her boots before stepping into the bright morning, squinting at the falling sunbeams, dust motes floating.

Iggy had crossed the clearing by the river, his feet treading the same path he'd taken so many times already, heading for the large sun-stone. It was not unlike a flat dais, the perfect place for him to draw strength. *We're all like plants but I'm more fragile, like a flower, I guess,* Iggy sometimes claimed.

And maybe it was true. What else explained receiving sustenance from sunlight?

Everyone in the village bore the same trait, to varying degrees, but for Iggy it was more than supplementary. It was *everything*. Somehow, his skin transformed sunlight into psychic and psychical energy at a far greater rate than anyone else. And watching him do it was still odd, something she should have been used to by now. Or maybe, it was still awe-inspiring. A little like when seeing him drink by submerging himself in water – hence his hut by the river.

At least, that was one reason.

Arun, the village Iemeda, had attempted to explain it all to Mei and the rest of the family, yet the complex process was beyond her understanding for the most part. But she knew how important sunlight was for everyone – and especially for Iggy – and how harsh the toll of winter and darkness could be on his body.

Her brother, aware of her presence, gave a wave before removing his tunic to stretch out on the rock, pale chest becoming luminescent in the light. High above him, a branch that had been half-broken cast a shadow across the sun-stone.

The air grew still and Mei skipped forward. "Let me," she said.

*I'm much calmer today, I'll be fine.*

"Just concentrate on the sun for now," Mei said.

Brushing aside the branch was not a difficult task. Mei's own telekinesis was strong, stronger than most in the village, even if beside her brother she was an infant. She stared up at the tree, blocked out the woods, the sounds of the birds and the water, even the sense of green and blue colours, until only the branch remained. Psychic force built swiftly. Her temples began to throb, but she released her power and the branch crashed into the trees.

*Very subtle, Mei.* He sounded quite amused.

Mei raised an eyebrow. "Well, at least I didn't knock a whole piece of mountain off. That probably sounds familiar to you, right?"

His laughter resounded in her mind, and she joined him in spite of herself. It was good to hear some joy from Iggy, even if it wasn't with her ears.

"You know, I should get back soon. I don't want to miss Denuko Gree. He'll have news of the outside world, maybe even more stories about Cresideth. Perhaps you could carve something to trade? He'd love your carvings, you know."

*Maybe tell Denuko next time. But come back and share whatever you learn when you can,* he added after a moment. *Especially if it is about the land of red sails.*

"Count on it." She started back to the hut to retrieve her cloak, pausing at the door. "Are you going to be all right?" The sunlight usually cheered him considerably, but each time he saw their mother, it took a little longer for him to forget.

*I will.*

Mei gathered her cloak and one of the walking sticks, then

started back through the trees.

Before she reached the road, she noticed an odd structure set off a little way from Iggy's home. Half-covered in shrubs and brambles, the shape of a keel was still clear. It was crudely fashioned and quite small but would probably float. Did Iggy plan to sail it along the river? Would he need help?

*Mei, thank you for last night too.* Iggy's voice echoed in her mind.

She smiled. "You're welcome."

## CHAPTER 3. – MEI

The circular, mud-brick houses and their blooming gardens of blue and pink were subdued, unusual for such a bright day. Few people were out. Old Finerma was scraping moth eggs from the wooden sill on the windows of her house, her movements stiff but determined. Up ahead, only the twins in their pale smocks. They were swinging sticks at the roof, leaping for a trapped ball.

The merchant passed through the Moon Gate only once a quarter and it usually caused an almost festival-like atmosphere to fall over the Inora. People should have been ready with sun-patterned weavings and other goods to sell. If the merchant had arrived, why was it so quiet? Mei called to the twins, but they scattered at her voice.

"Hey, what's wrong?" she called after them but they did not stop.

And Finerma was shuffling back inside, closing her door to leave only its painted orchid for Mei to address, and it would hardly answer any questions.

Mei frowned as she set off at a jog, slipping through the trellises of her garden, dragging in the scent of rose as she did, and peered into the window. An empty kitchen and the curves that obscured both bedrooms seemingly empty, too. "Mother?"

No reply.

Leaning against the brick a moment, Mei listened. Usually, the sound of laughter would assault her ears – visiting cousins chasing butterflies in the garden, calls from the neighbours and the ring of hammer on steel or, come noon, chants of the Paragons from the Village Oratory.

None of it! And on a day when Denuko might arrive. What was happening?

She pushed on the door. "Mother, is everything all right?"

Empty.

Nothing was out of place inside. The walls were still decorated with flowers, and chairs had been pushed beneath the table, water jug perfectly centred. A loaf of spiced pajen-bread sat wrapped in cloth. She smiled. Hardly like her own room; it looked more like Ig was still around.

But the bedrooms were empty too, and no-one was hiding in the rumpled blankets of her bed.

Mei ran back outside as her pulse quickened. Something was wrong.

Up ahead, an old man in a green robe walked toward the Village Oratory, its windowed dome ringed by twin decks, the murmur of voices slipping from multiple entries. "Arun, where is everyone?" she called to him.

The village Iemeda waved her closer and a chill fell over Mei when she saw his face. The wrinkles around his eyes and mouth were set in lines of grief. His white hair was tinged with pollen and the familiar sight ought to have brought a smile to her face, but the look in his eyes...

"Meiaja." He reached out to place his hands upon her shoulders. "The village is meeting to discuss your brother's fate."

"Again? Wasn't the last time enough?"

"Mei –"

She shook free, voice raised. "No, Arun! What else can they do to him? Isn't it enough that they have him living out in the woods like a beast?" She opened her mouth to take a breath, meaning to continue, but Arun raised a finger.

"Garid nearly died."

Mei blinked. "How?"

His jaw tightened. "Iggy's anger. The hole he tore through the walls of the inn after... speaking with your mother. One of the bricks nearly crushed Garid's ribcage and he lies near death in my home even now. I left Ki with him. Everyone else is no doubt at the meeting."

Mei pushed down her concern for Garid – he was a good man... but the whole village deciding Iggy's fate without including him? Far too callous. "Even my mother, I suppose. Leading the pack."

Arun frowned. "That's not true."

"Isn't it?"

"No. Siratta is just as upset as Iggy." He paused at the steps leading up to the veranda.

Mei extended a hand to help Arun up onto the decking. "I'll believe that when I see it, Iemeda."

A bleak hush fell over the hall, clear on the faces and even the walls – all the flower-wreaths had been taken down, replaced by carven statuettes of the Guiding Ones in their stern poses, arms folded or gripping the Tenants of Wisdom. Their unforgiving poses were matched by the ring of Paragons.

Each man and woman stood in their green robes that covered even boots and sandals, standing on the dais at regular intervals before the rest of the Inora. Mei looked for her mother as she and Arun joined the circle.

There, standing beside Paragon Mikal.

Gripping Mikal's hand, her green eyes red-rimmed. Her long hair was tied into a bun and she stood rigid in the same grey skirts she'd worn during Iggy's visit. Mei met her mother's gaze, glaring. And even though they wouldn't be heard, she mouthed the words, 'He doesn't deserve this, and you know it.'

Siratta looked away first and Mei continued to stare until Arun touched her shoulder, drawing her attention to what Paragon Mikal was saying.

The man's voice spread across the hall, tone firm but not harsh. It was a pleasant voice, the kind that children sat around for, demanding more stories. He drew every eye in the room as he listed the transgressions Iggy had committed over the years.

All unintentional, he was careful to stipulate, and Mei had to admit, some of the accidents *were* severe. Her hand went unconsciously to a scar on her thigh. There had been one winter where Ig's explosive power tore the rooves from several homes. Or the harvest where he was responsible for a terrible fire in the wheat fields.

But *none* of it meant he was a monster, some creature whose fate could be decided in his absence.

Something tugged on her skirt and she looked down – one of the twins; it was Hishi's small hand gripping the fabric. Mei smiled just enough to set her fury to one side for a moment. Behind the blonde-haired girl stood her sister Hisha, her own hair closer to red, and a small group of other children, most of them fidgeting. "We want to go and play," Hishi explained. "This is boring."

"Quietly, then," Mei said, and slipped from the circle, leading the giggling children to a back door, ignoring the occasional glance or glare from the villagers. "Have fun and don't go far."

Returning to her place beside Arun, Mei focused on Mikal. The Paragon had finally exhausted his list and was now offering his recommendation. "Due to the unpredictable and repeated nature of such unfortunate threats, I think the safest course of action, for Nokema and young Iggy, who we all must acknowledge suffers when he commits these acts..." He paused to look at Siratta. "... I fear it would be best for him to go into Exile of the Valley."

"No!" Mei stepped out of the circle. Gasps followed her and she spun on the people. "Protocol be damned. He would never survive that – the winter alone could kill him. How can we decide this for him? Surely, he has a right to be present?"

Paragon Pirael spoke. "We decided –"

"To wait until I was gone too, right?" Mei snapped.

The Paragons muttered among themselves, and she heard Garid's father cursing Iggy, but she ignored it all. Mikal glanced at Arun before speaking. "Your devotion to your brother is to be commended, Meiaja. But this is not a place for emotion, we must–"

"Pretending to be free of emotion doesn't make this the right thing to do."

Mikal raised both hands. "Please, Mei."

Siratta spoke. "Paragon Mikal, if I may?"

He nodded and Siratta looked down to Mei. "Mei, I love your brother, you know that." Her voice wavered, and for a moment her eyes blazed. "But I know what it is like when he loses control. I know. And so should you! How can I do nothing when it could happen to anyone at any time? Garid might not survive, don't you understand?"

"And that wouldn't have happened if you'd just forgive him for Father's death."

Siratta's face turned ashen grey, matching her dress. Tears built but her voice was steady, as though holding back the threat of emotion. "You are speaking out of turn, daughter."

Mei frowned at Siratta's reaction... maybe Mother did care after all? Something about it seemed to suggest that she *wanted* to forgive him. Hands fell upon Mei's shoulders, and Arun pulled her gently back into the ring of hushed villagers.

Mikal raised his voice. "Now that order has been restored, I will ask to hear from the Paragons first." He directed a stern look to Mei. "Will any offer other recommendations?"

Mei looked at the faces of those in green robes. Most shook their heads, but Garid's father, Galarik, raised a hand. "I do. It is my recommendation that Iggy be sent not into Exile of the Valley, but that he is Banished altogether, that he leave the Inora and lives beyond the Moon Gate."

Murmurs filled the Oratory at his words. Mei spun to Arun, then her mother. If Exile of the Valley was a death sentence for Iggy, Banishment was a hundred times worse. Not only would it seal his death, but the dishonour...

"Mother, this is wrong!" Mei shouted.

Other voices rose; agreement – even cheers from some, and Mei swallowed back tears. They didn't understand!

Arun lifted both arms, his rasping voice urging for quiet over the rising din. In time, the villagers hushed for the most part. The healer turned to his fellow Paragon. "I understand your grief, Galarik, but I urge against this. The memory of Tasaja, a great man, should not be stained thus, nor should Siratta and Mei have to bear it. I will therefore cast my vote now, against this."

"So be it," Galarik nodded, but his face remained hard.

Mikal gestured to the remaining Paragons. "Paragon Arun has opened the vote. We now vote on the Banishment of Igija, Son of Tasaja. If it is defeated, we will vote on Exile of the Valley."

Mei swallowed as the voting began. If they voted on Banishment, she'd find Iggy first.

And yet, the vote was swift. Of the seven Paragons, only two other Paragons voted for Banishment, Garid's mother and also Seer Egril. Mei sneered when Egril voted; it was no surprise. Jealousy had long lingered, seemingly over Siratta and Tasaja's marriage.

But some of the tension slipped from Mei's limbs, nevertheless.

"Very well, now we vote on the –" Mikal stopped at a commotion from one of the entryways. Ki pounded into the Hall, her face pale and eyes wide. There were even leaves in her braids. "Forgive me, but it is Garid."

Galarik strode across the room, his wife in tow. "Tell us."

"I'm sorry, Paragon. He fought hard, but he has returned to the sun," the young woman said, averting her gaze.

Mei flinched.

And yet Galarik did not leap through the window and charge off to Ig's hut. The man only comforted his wife, Nifra, who had collapsed into his arms. The Paragon started to walk her back to their place in the circle when he stopped.

"I demand we vote again. On Banishment."

"No!" Mei cried.

Mikal stepped forward to shout over the clamour that followed Galarik's words. "That is not permitted."

Galarik gently untangled himself from Nifra and looked directly at Mei. "Then I will deliver justice myself."

A child's scream tore through the air.

In the stunned silence that followed, a second scream rang out. "Where are the children?" someone shouted.

Almost as one, the villagers charged the exits.

Somehow, Mei pushed her way through the bodies to a rear door, sprinting along the paved stones toward her home and the back garden. Hishi, Hisha and the others would likely be playing there; they loved hopping games.

But she'd barely covered half the distance before thudding to a halt.

From the south, somewhere within the waving sea of golden wheat, came the growls of Blood Cats.

# CHAPTER 4. – CINDER

The man tied to the cross glared down at a pair of Royal Nasaru soldiers where they stood in their red cloaks. It was a shame he couldn't burn holes in their bladders with his eyes.

But Cinder was no sorcerer.

Just a thief – and quite a good one too, even if being caught obviously contradicted the fact. Something black fluttered near Cinder's head. He twitched as a raven landed on his wrist, its black feathers almost oily in the sun that beat upon his stubbled face, harsh enough to having him squinting, sweating and parched all at once.

Cinder huffed and puffed at the bird, wincing as claws dug into his skin. Useless, of course, and such ineffectual efforts to keep the raven away seemed to amuse it, as it let out a long croak and hopped closer.

Dust swirled around the crossroads, but it could not mask the faint scent of ripe plums, which drifted from the nearby orchard. It bordered the Omaila Forest but was yet another place controlled by the Royal Family, off-limits save for those permitted to toil away for pennies within.

Black feathers twitched at the edge of his vision.

"Why don't you surprise me and help me out, lads?" he asked the guards, who leant against their mounts and jeered.

"Worried he'll peck out your eyes, thief?" The older one nudged his fellow as he spoke, breastplate gleaming.

Cinder frowned. "My sentence is starvation and death by exposure, and that's what I've come to terms with. Being eaten alive by birds was not on the cards, I have to say." Cinder tried to turn his face from the looming beak, but the bindings on his forehead were too tight.

"We don't control the birds, sonny," the other one said, his long moustache half-concealing a smirk.

"Thank you for that information, *father.*"

The guard straightened, hand on his sword hilt.

The older man caught his arm. "We've done our bit, Hedn."

"Fine." He started to mount up.

The raven croaked again. Cinder glared at the black blob of feathers... and beyond, a grey shape appeared, moving up the road. Mounted on a large roan was a broad-shouldered man in a grey cloak and hood. All that was visible of him were his dark hands on the reins which, Cinder noted when the man brought the horse to a halt nearby, were adorned by a single ring of amethyst.

"What's a Greyshield doing here?" Hedn muttered, stepping out of his stirrup and coming to attention.

Cinder blinked. Officially, Greyshields were Lords and Ladies of the King's Court, skilful soldiers or politicians. Unofficially, some were assassins. Men and women who had been trained in hidden camps since they were old enough to run, feared across the lands... hard to say how true it all was. Even the City's Cloak were hardly aware of their movements.

What could it mean that one was here?

Intriguing... at least, it would be had he not been tied to a cross.

From the corner of Cinder's eye, the raven lunged – its beak gashing his cheek. He swore as warm blood trickled down his throat. "Can someone do something about this bloody bird!"

The Greyshield moved his head, a slight creasing of the hood, and the raven exploded in a puff of feathers. Cinder blinked. Spotting sleight of hand was his bread and butter but he hadn't even seen the rider's hand move, let alone what was thrown.

"You men, why do you loiter here?" The voice that issued from the hood was deep and strong, but it was not raised.

Cinder snickered as Hedn and the other guard snapped to attention. "My Lord, we were just leaving. The prisoner has been sentenced –"

"Justice does not need a wet-nurse."

The soldiers bowed before mounting up and kicking their horses into a canter, leaving only smudges of dust hanging over the highway.

The grey-clothed man resumed his ride, passing Cinder without looking up.

"My Lord, thank you," Cinder said. "If you grant me another mercy, might I repay you in some way?"

"It is unlikely."

Had there been a trace of amusement in the voice? Time to throw the dice anyway – or hurl them forth, actually. "No doubt I hold little interest to a lord such as yourself, but I believe I know what you seek."

The Greyshield halted and turned his horse. Stopping

beneath the cross now, he pushed his hood back. Green eyes glittered from a hard face. Short black hair, dusted silver at the temples, contrasted with his dark skin, and his beard was closely cropped. "Do you, now?"

"I believe I have information worth an escort to the border, at least."

"You would bargain with me? That shows some nerve for a common criminal. And look where it got you...?"

He grinned. "Cinder, My Lord. And begging your pardon, but only the best criminals are sent here to starve, in full view of the public."

A moment of silence before the Greyshield waved a hand. "Impress me, thief."

"I recently returned from Takirov, where I came across a letter in a man's purse. Something that would interest you, My Lord. High treason and such."

"Give the letter to me."

"Well, after memorising it, I burnt it. In fact, I was on my way to inform the proper authorities when I was collected by the City Cloak."

"A concerned citizen."

"Some days, I can be. But it was a misunderstanding; I was simply caught between the guard and an unsavoury fellow who was inquiring after the purchase of human labour."

The Greyshield's eyes narrowed. "Slavery is prohibited in Nasaru."

"Indeed," Cinder replied. "But as I was saying, it was a misunderstanding – I am no comrade of that filthy slaver."

"And yet here you are."

"No-one believed me, of course. That's why I need your help.

I can't show my face in Omaila again now, so I thought I'd head for one of the borders. You could safeguard my passage. No-one would question a Greyshield."

"True, no-one would," the lord replied. "Yet I am not convinced."

"I will share the entire letter once we reach a border. It doesn't have to be across the nation either. The Valley of the Inora is not out of reach, for instance, and I'm sure it wouldn't inconvenience you much."

"Give me something from the letter."

"Asaro Itonye," Cinder said.

The Greyshield's eyes widened ever-so-slightly. "Few people beyond the court know of that name."

"Yes, My Lord."

He dismounted, retrieved a water flask from his pack and took hold of the lower wing of the cross – climbing quickly to tip water into Cinder's parched mouth.

Cinder swallowed greedily. "Thank you." He gasped, relief causing him to close his eyes with a sigh.

The lord began to climb down.

"Aren't you going to free me?" Cinder cried.

"Wait here," the man said as he returned to his horse and raised his hood, tapping the flanks of his mount.

"What?"

"It may be a day before I can return," he replied without turning. "Try to stay lucid."

"A day?" Cinder swore as he struggled against his bonds. What was the lord's game? *The bastard is gambling with my life.* "Fine! Don't be so sure I'll be here when you do – I hope I'm dead!" he shouted.

## CHAPTER 5. – ROKURA

Lord Rokura, King's Greyshield, nobleman and widower, raised his head at a new sound in the dark of the forest.

His mount, Arrow, waited back at camp, concealed within a hollow set off the highway. The sound was not his horse, no. The trail of the Takirova rebels led him to this point, having circled around their likely path. They'd been hiding well enough, but a large group would always leave clear evidence of their passage.

Rokura parted the leaves, the cool scent of mint mixed in the loam.

There. Faint light and a clanking sound drifted from between entwined trunks. *Finally.* His patience had paid off. And since encountering Cinder, it had taken a little extra effort to wait in place, to remain focused on his task.

Asaro Itonye.

Few were aware of that name indeed.

But *if* the thief had spoken the truth, it might well explain the purpose of the Takirova, sneaking throughout Nasaru lands and abducting villagers.

And there were more than a few villages in the forest of

Omaila; after all, the place was tame compared to the wild masses of the Crawling Woods in Cresideth or the poisonous clutches of Senoja's Kaavi Wood. Omaila was more beautiful. Frequented by parties of nobles riding out from their vacation estates, the forest actually lay sprinkled with parks and secret pools where lovers would meet.

Impractical, of course, but it was ever the want of youth to seek privacy... so, too, for older nobles who had much to hide. And to escape the prying eyes of the court, sometimes such measures did not seem extreme in the slightest.

But this new sound was hard and steely, not the whispers or laughter of drunken voices. Besides which, spring nights so far this year seemed too chilly for lovers' trysts or parties.

Rokura opened his grey cloak and took up a shielded lantern, drawing a thin blade from its sheath with barely a hiss. He followed the clank of steel on steel deeper into the forest, sliding past fragrant shrubs and gliding across moon-lit clearings until he came upon a game trail at the bottom of a gully.

From the other side of the steep rise now came more steel against steel, small sounds like hilts against armour. Setting his lantern down, Rokura climbed to the spur and peered over a fallen log, forearms sinking into the moss.

A line of people slithered along the gully floor. They numbered twenty or so by his quick count, stretching back to another rise where lanterns from the guards gave away their position via brief flashes of colour.

Rokura's hand tightened around the handle of his blade, eyes roving over the shadowed faces of men, women and children – over half the number of prisoners were children.

Their passage was hampered by bindings on their hands, each child tied to the next. The adults did not seem bound to the children, but the Takirova rebels were well-armed, if the rear guard was anything to go by.

The other overseers were spaced at regular intervals, but harder to see clearly. And while there was no sense the adults were going to attempt an escape, the Takirova were keeping a close watch. When one woman stumbled into a rebel, the man struck her across the face. She fell to her knees, then toppled over. A fellow prisoner bent at her side but was hauled up quickly. The children nearest began to struggle and muffled cries slipped forth – were they all gagged too?

From the front of the line came a single word in the Takirova tongue, issued from a figure who stood head and shoulders taller than the rest. "Continue."

And the line did not stop for the woman.

Rokura's jaw tightened, yet he did not strike. The risk of casualties among the prisoners was too high – at least five or six rebels walked within the line, and their path would be easy to follow once they passed. The woman needed help, whether she would be able to provide information about her captors or not.

*A little more patience.*

He'd likely found evidence of the very plot the king had sent him to discover, but *who* lurked behind it? Were any in Takirov so organised? Even among the various groups of malcontents? Were they getting assistance from a familiar enemy, perhaps? *Is Senoja moving again?*

Speculation only.

In any event, picking off rebels one by one, leaving the

vanguard until last was also possible... but information had to come first. Capturing at least one rebel without being noticed also seemed unlikely, based on their positions. And any interrogations would require privacy to conduct.

To land the bigger fish, he needed more information.

Confirmation of their purpose and destination, at least.

Reports of rebels striking Makiya in Takirov and villages along the borders of the Barrenhome, even coastal parts of Nasaru, had been dismissed as isolated events. King Mutolo believed them disorganised and random, even as he dispatched reinforcements to existing garrisons.

His Greyshields were not sent... at first.

Now, it was swiftly becoming clear something large was afoot. Was the old colony planning to finally push the lingering remnants of Nasaru governance from its lands? The king was loath to give up the precious Black Coral and the levies he imposed upon them...

Of course, the man devoted equal rhetoric – or sincere concern – to protecting citizens. Yet, it was not always clear which words the king *felt* and which he merely delivered as per his role.

*Enough pondering.* The column had wound its way out of sight now, continuing on a southern course away from the capital. And eventually, toward Takirov? When the last glimpse of light disappeared, Rokura retrieved his lantern and slipped down to the gully floor, searching for the prisoner.

Laboured breathing led him to her side.

An older woman with specks of blood in her greying hair lay twisted at the foot of a mighty elm. Her clothes were ripped in several places, her arms and legs covered with bruises.

A trickle of blood flowed from her mouth and her eyes widened when he knelt. "Quietly," he cautioned as he examined her body. "I will help you."

"My grandson," she whispered.

"Save your strength a little longer." He lifted her easily. Bandages and medicine waited at his camp, water and food… and while it might not be enough to save her, his duty was clear.

And more.

Once the poor woman had been restored and taken to the nearest Wayside Inn, depending on what she could share, it was probably time to return to the Orchard Crossroads to collect a thief named Cinder.

It was not so far, after all.

And the truth behind the name Asaro Itonye *had* to be solved. For what appeared to be a group of rebels taking Nasaru hostages from isolated villages might indeed be something much more serious…

## CHAPTER 6. – MEI

Mei sprinted, and it seemed her feet didn't touch the ground as the homes flashed by. All sounds from the village had been sucked into a muted void, whisked away by the panic that drove her limbs.

Only the thump of her heart remained – a riot within her chest.

It had been years since the Blood Cats came north from their dens beyond the Wheat Fields. Why now? *And why didn't we sense their approach?* Mei leapt over a low hedge of white roses, tearing her pant leg on the thorns but not slowing.

When the Blood Cats last appeared, Mei had been a typical Inora child, hardly able to direct her telekinetic powers – her cousins would not be exceptions. Had Ren been with the children? A little younger than Ig, Ren might be able to hold the cats off... if there weren't too many.

From the east, the screaming had stopped, replaced by shouts and howls from the south now, as the adults attacked the Blood Cats. *Good.*

And finally, home appeared ahead.

Mei skidded around the side of the house and burst into

her garden.

A black, fur-covered creature, almost the size of a pony, crouched over one of the girls.

Long whiskers twitched as it lifted its head, yellow eyes blazing. A guttural sound burst from its throat as Mei stepped closer, her jaw clenched, fists too. Ren was pressed against the wall, shielding the rest of the children as best he could. His eyes were wide as he gestured in frantic sweeps.

Thorns flew from rose bushes, only to bounce off the Blood Cat's thick fur.

But when one struck the cat's face, it flinched back several steps.

Mei reached out with her mind and rolled the girl toward Ren, who caught on right away. His own telekinesis brushed against Mei, a trembling energy, but enough to draw the little one closer.

Mei swallowed. Was it Hishi or Hisha?

And was that blood on her dress?

The Blood Cat hissed. Mei spun. She sent an invisible bolt of psychic energy into the creature's chest with a grunt. Bones cracked. The cat howled as it collapsed and Mei struck again, snapping a foreleg. She couldn't help but wince.

But there was no time for mercy.

"Get her to the Iemeda, Ren," Mei said. "Everyone else inside, now."

The older boy rushed forward to scoop up the girl – it was Hishi – the rest of the children scrambling around and toward the front door, most with whimpers and Hisha with tears streaming down her cheeks.

But Mei kept her eyes on the huge cat, the throbbing in

her temples not enough to distract her, even as the pain grew. And despite twisted growls from the Blood Cat, it was not finished.

It crouched, snarling.

"Don't," Mei said.

But the beast leapt, powerful hind legs driving it through the air. Mei lashed out again, and a deep crunch followed.

The Blood Cat crashed down at her feet with a thud. Grass seeds caught in its dark fur and saliva glistened in a gaping mouth but the huge cat did not move, its throat crushed. A surge of triumph clashed with revulsion. And not just at scent of blood from the animal... from the act of violence. Yet, the Blood Cat *had* to be killed. To protect the village.

"Mei, there's another one!"

Mei spun to the where one of the children pointed from the window.

Another large beast pushed through the hedge, eyes aglow, whiskers twitching.

She hurled forth yet another blast at the new Blood Cat and it retreated only momentarily, resuming its approach all too soon.

Not enough power.

Mei's vision was already darkening. *No!* The pain within her temples built in a tremendous pressure, as though her skull had been caught in a vice. She'd pushed too hard, attacking too often in a short period of time.

Her knees gave way, and she collapsed to the ground, supporting herself with trembling arms. Somehow, she managed to speak, voice seeming distant. "Where is it? What direction is –"

Something sharp and hot ripped into her shoulder.

The blow sent her tumbling into the hedge. She must have cried out, surely, but her senses offered nothing. Branches dug into her back, and those should have hurt, but the pain was dulled, another bad sign. *Where is it? Where?*

Surging panic forced her into a roll, with no clues as to the Blood Cat's nearness, nor even what direction she'd moved… but her desperate act wasn't going to make a difference.

Her limbs no longer responded.

"Iggy!"

She screamed his name but the darkness came for her.

***

Mei woke to find Paragon Arun smiling down at her, his white hair gleaming in warm candlelight.

"What…?" Blankets had been pulled up around her neck where she lay in the Iemeda's adjoining rooms. She blinked rapidly as her other senses returned. Every bit of her skin was chilled, a contrast to the crackle of a nearby fire. The scent of eucalyptus was strong; that, and painkiller and healing herbs.

She tried to sit up but the blankets were too tight, and a dull throb from her shoulder caused her to wince – bandaged. Worse, her slight movements caused ripples of pain to ravage her head, too. She closed her eyes and whispered. "The children?"

Silence.

She squinted now.

Arun was holding a cup, which he lifted to her lips. "Drink first."

Mei did as instructed. The sweet liquid stung, but it eased her discomfort and she slowly became aware of others in the room, several figures standing at the edge of the firelight. Mother and Aunt Wifral, both with tear-streaked faces. Aunt Wifral's hair was in disarray, free from its usual braid.

Beside them in turn waited Paragon Mikal and Ren. Ren's far smaller hands were white-knuckled, wrapped around his mug – no doubt more of Arun's medicine.

"Tell me, please. What about Hishi and Hisha? The others?"

At Mei's question, Wifral let out a sob. Siratta took her hand, murmuring softly. Mei tried to sit up again, as her mother began to lead the woman from the house. "What happened?"

Aunt Wifral spun. "How could you let them leave the hall? Hishi is dead! And it's your fault, you stupid, stupid girl."

Mei flinched.

Candles dimmed and the air crackled with power but Paragon Mikal stood and spoke a word of command.

The threat of Aunt Wifral's telekinesis disappeared.

Had she actually been close to attacking?

A moment of silence passed as Wifral and Mikal locked gazes, but she soon turned away with a hiss. Nodding to Arun, Paragon Mikal ushered the distraught woman from the room. Siratta followed.

"Arun, tell me." Hishi... How could that little girl be gone? She was so sweet and kind, always the first to share her fruit or the flowers she found, anything really. Tears stung Mei's eyes. *And there is no-one else to blame.* She made a fist beneath the blankets.

Arun turned to face Ren, whose eyes were wide. "You were very brave today, Ren. Go now and try to sleep. Mei is well, as you can see."

Ren looked up and flushed. "O-Of course, Iemeda. Thank you," he stammered, trying to smile at Mei as he left.

The healer turned back to her. "He was quite insistent that he see you. You saved Ren and the other children, you know."

Mei swallowed back more tears. "But not Hishi."

He sat beside her, stroking her hair. "No, my dear. But it is very likely that she was already gone when you arrived. *No-one* could have saved her. And you could not have done more."

"But I *did* let them outside to play." Tears slid down her face and onto the pillow, leaving behind cold trails as they fell. What would Hisha do now? She and Hishi were inseparable. "How can I face them?"

"Your aunt is grieving. You are not to blame, Mei."

"But –"

"You did not call the Blood Cats here. That is an undeniable fact."

"But I let the children out, Arun," Mei said, her voice wavering. "That's also the truth."

"The children would have asked someone else, had you not been there. Let's say, Tiralin. If that had happened, would you have blamed Tiralin?"

"No."

"Then be kind to yourself now."

Mei closed her eyes, and waiting for her in what should have been darkness was Hishi's smiling face, a smudge of pollen on her cheek. "I know what you're trying to do, Iemeda... but that's just not how I feel."

"Perhaps we have taxed you needlessly," he said, regret plain in his voice. He rose, disappearing into the shadows a moment. The clink of a spoon against a cup followed and when he returned, he held another mug, this one filled with a steaming liquid with a more acrid aroma. "Drink this and rest, Mei. It's been a long few days and your body is still recovering."

Mei drew in a faint breath. "Few days?"

"Yes. Three. We were all quite terrified, the first night." He held the warm cup to her mouth. "Now drink and rest. We will talk again when you wake."

She gulped it down, the unpleasant taste contrasting with a comforting heat... but as much as sleep would be welcome, as much as any escape from guilt would be welcome, she had one more question to ask.

Arun had continued speaking. "The Blood Cat's saliva gave you a fever with its poison. It broke in the early hours of the second night, and now you just have to ride out the chill it causes. We took turns watching over you, even Paragon Mikal. On top of that, of course, you'd already pushed yourself too far, I've no doubt. But your body is finally mending itself."

A pleasant lethargy crept over Mei as she listened, and the candlelight began to bloom and waver, yet she managed to ask her question with just a whisper. "Who stopped the second Cat?"

"Your brother."

## CHAPTER 7. – MEI

"So, Iggy saved me?" Mei sat in her own bed now, sunlight and the scent of rose both slipping through the open window. And it might have been the sun as much as Arun's medicines that gave her limbs a new energy, with even her shoulder feeling significantly better. However, her recovery could not be total.

Hishi was still gone.

*And nothing can change that.*

Arun had needed to move her back home, since space for other victims of the attack was limited.

According to Siratta, the Blood Cats fell upon Nokema in force. The Paragons estimated that at least four separate families had been involved in an attack, which was unheard of in size. Blood Cats had plenty of game to the south, and incidents in the past had *always* been the work of a lone creature.

An ill omen.

Had the Cats been forced north by something? Villagers had already been dispatched to investigate, Galarik among them. The first night, one of the older children had reported seeing a pale, shimmering shape on the outskirts of the village but what could that have meant?

"Yes, it was Iggy," Arun said as he paced slowly before the foot of her bed, hands behind his back, green robe bright in the noon sun. "I spoke with him after, only briefly. I still believe he must have been close to the village already... otherwise, it hardly makes sense."

"What do you mean?"

Arun paused. "Well… Iggy claimed that he flew here."

"Flew?"

"He said he didn't understand himself. I should say, he called it 'flying' for a lack of another term. I doubt even Iggy knows how he arrived in time." Arun spread wrinkled hands. "He was working on something when he felt our battle with the Blood Cats. He left immediately but when he heard your cry, something came over him. He gathered the light and suddenly he was here, in the village. At least, that's how he described what happened."

She shook her head slowly, leaning back against the pillow. "It that even possible? In all the Inora's history?"

"I am trying to discover just that."

Mei massaged her temples gently. "Siratta said that other families were attacked. Are they hurt?"

"Siratta?" Arun said with a frown.

"I'll call her 'Mother' again when she starts acting like one," Mei replied, keeping her tone even as best she could.

The Iemeda sighed. "I'll move on then, shall I? Iggy probably saved Nokema; I have never seen its like. He was a whirlwind. Simply everywhere whenever he was needed, and so other injuries were comparatively light. Comparatively, at least."

Arun did not continue at once, his grey eyes troubled. "But his power shook the earth, Mei. A thing of awe *and* terror.

And when he drove them off – and dozens of the Blood Cats had come – he left fully half their number in bloody pieces, shattered where they fell."

*Shattered?* She straightened, hope overpowering both relief *and* concern at the description of Iggy's power. "Then he saved us. It's obvious, isn't it? Surely now Paragon Mikal and the others will reconsider..." She trailed off at the expression on the old man's face. "Where is Ig now?"

"I do not know. The vote was taken while he chased the Blood Cats beyond the wheat fields."

"And?"

The old man stopped, facing the window. "Only I voted against it."

Mei gaped into the silence. Even after Iggy saved the entire village... even *that* was not enough? "Cowards," she finally managed.

"Do not judge them too harshly, Mei. They do what they believe is best –"

She cast the blankets aside. "Best for the village, yes. I've heard it all before, Arun."

Arun's face hardened. "I think it best that I wish you a speedy recovery now, young lady. I have other patients to check on," he said as he strode from the room, heading for the front door.

Mei hesitated at a flash of shame. Calling him back to apologise shouldn't have been so hard... and he was not a deserving target for her outburst, not in any way, but all her life she had heard about what was best for the village and no-one had ever asked to hear what Ig wanted. No-one had tried to help him, not truly.

"I'll visit him." Her strength was almost back to normal, and her headache was faint now; nothing an hour's walk in the sun couldn't take care of.

Iggy would be home. He would have simply ignored the decision of the village, if he'd even heard it. And no-one was strong enough to force him to leave anyway. He was probably lying on his sun-stone and laughing at them... Or maybe fighting back bitter tears at yet another rejection from a bunch of ungrateful fools.

Mei hopped out of bed with a curse at a twinge of pain in her shoulder. Tossing the blankets aside had aggravated the wound from the Blood Cat. She probed it gently; still healing, after all. And when she stepped into a skirt it wasn't without some effort.

"What are you doing, Mei?" Siratta stood in the doorway, expression one of concern. She set an armful of greens upon the cold stove. "You shouldn't be out of bed, let me help you. Are you thirsty?" Her face was weary but her voice gentle as she smiled at her daughter and moved forward, wrapping Mei in an embrace.

Mei could not answer.

It was all too sudden, the tenderness.

Siratta's scent of crushed grapes was so familiar... Mei closed her eyes a moment. Just like the days when father was still alive. How different to the usual resentment. And Mei had to admit, it was all too easy to forget Siratta's strength. Here she was, exhausted from grief but still on her feet, still working barely three days after an attack on the entire village where her daughter was wounded, her niece killed, and her son Banished.

"I would like some water, thank you," Mei squeezed her mother as she let her head rest on the woman's shoulder. Siratta stroked Mei's hair and the pain in her arm receded a moment. "The Guardians were watching over you, Meiaja. Sit down a moment; I want to talk with you."

Mei sat and waited for the water her mother brought. "Has something else happened?" she asked after a long drink.

Siratta held her gaze. "This will be difficult to hear, but you have to be strong."

"What is it?"

"After Mikal told Iggy about the Banishment, I spoke to him." She took both Mei's hands now. "I told him that I loved him, but that I thought it best he left us."

Mei jerked free. "What? How could you do that? You're supposed to be his *mother*."

Siratta's hand flashed.

Mei reeled back from a ringing slap upon her face. Not the pain, but the sting of betrayal. She placed a hand over the hot part of her cheek. Just moments ago, Siratta had embraced her, something she hadn't done in years, and now this?

Her mother's gaze didn't waver. "I am a mother to both my children, Mei. I love Iggy and I only want to protect him."

"How is that even remotely true?"

Siratta raised her voice. "Galarik and Egril were talking about banding together and casting your brother into the Void beneath the Gate! Mikal and the others would have opposed it, but who knew Garid would die? Banishment was the only way to save Iggy's life, do you understand? At least now, he may live in peace beyond Nokema."

Mei slumped; anger rushed out of her.

The Void beneath the tunnels… the *Nenos*.

A place reserved for Inora that committed the most heinous crimes.

Built deep into a chamber located beneath the Dalma Mountains, it was an unfathomable well. Only the Paragons knew precisely where it was, but most of the Inora described it as being near the passage to the Otherlands, in the west. Some said it was actually beside the Moon Gate but only the Paragons were permitted to escort such criminals to the Void.

Wherever it lay, it was no place worth seeking, since it nullified any and all psychic power. Even those incredibly few that were said to have climbed back out were not only powerless, but mad, empty people. Before Ig was born, Mei saw one. Galarik eventually ran the man out of the village and across the river, but she remembered the criminal's dirty face and the bird-skull he whispered to, the hopelessly dead eyes.

"I can't believe that. Even of Galarik and Egril."

Her mother's expression did not change. "Arun told me himself."

"But Iggy doesn't mean it, you know that. He isn't evil, he's just…" Mei struggled for a word.

"Dangerous," Siratta said, folding her arms. "It's time you admitted it, Mei. Ig is dangerous and even he knows it beyond any doubt now."

Mei narrowed her eyes. "What does that mean?"

"He wept as I held him," Siratta said as she looked away. "For the first time since they sent him to the woods… but he knows we are afraid of him."

Mei lifted her chin. "Maybe you and the others, but I'm not."

"He agreed with me, Mei. Iggy himself thinks it is the right thing to do." She paused. "I think maybe he wanted to go."

Mei froze. "That's a lie."

"He gave me a message. For you," Siratta said. "Will you hear it?"

She nodded, unable to speak.

"Iggy said he loves you. He asked, would you try to be happy for him. He's going to take care of himself now; he wants to be strong like his sister."

Hot tears built swiftly and Mei's throat closed up, but she couldn't prevent a sob. Her mother embraced her again, still talking. "Ig says he owes his life to you and that he wants to give you yours back."

"He was never a burden, Mother," she whispered.

"I know that. He wasn't angry, Mei. He seemed to be at peace. Be happy for him, darling, please."

Mei couldn't answer.

## CHAPTER 8. – MEI

It took much longer than usual to reach Iggy's hut.

At full strength, running half the distance would not have been impossible. But now, even her plodding steps sent jolts of pain up Mei's bandaged arm. The late-spring sun on her back had helped with the climb, but she was still sweating and breathing hard when she finally came to a halt at the door.

And even before she pushed open the wood, Mei knew he was gone. His home had an empty feel, even from the outside.

More telling, there was no sense of his power nearby.

"Iggy."

Inside, everything was in order. As though he was due to return by nightfall. He'd even cleared the stove pot of ash and straightened the bed. Mei slumped down and sucked in a breath. New tension was replacing her weariness. "Where are you going?" She beat a fist into the mattress of pine needles.

Something dropped onto the bed and she turned.

A statuette had fallen from the small bedside table. She lifted it, the pine soft and cool in her palm. A young man in a cloak; his hair wild and his face wearing a broad smile. Mei recognised him, even with the eyes, nose and mouth – almost like a young image of Father.

Her chest grew tight as she stood, placing the carving into a tunic pocket as she left.

"Is he…?" Where would Iggy find someone to give him a face?

*Just like him to dream big. And just like him to want to do it alone.*

Outside, she crossed the grassy earth to the sun-stone. How many times had she visited to find him there? She stretched across it herself, closing her eyes and imagining him sitting beside her, his bare back gleaming where the rays had been unable to tan his skin. A cloud passed over the sun and Mei shivered.

He'd be in danger out there, without her help. His body wasn't strong enough. At least summer was close; he'd never survive a winter alone. Mei opened her eyes. Green needles on the branches of surrounding trees were black against the blue sky and she sat up, a new chill enveloping her.

*What about me?*

Siratta had made her decision, and she had Mikal. Arun had Ki to help him... and the village? Well, they didn't care. She was a thorn in their side, always challenging them when it came to her brother.

And now, after Hishi's death, no-one would want to see her, anyway.

A faint sound reached her.

From the pines? Slipping down, she approached the tree line with narrowed eyes. *Did I imagine it?* The river murmured beneath the chattering of birds but had it been the faint thud of footsteps on the road?

Yet, peering through the tree trunks offered no answer.

The boat!

Mei surged forward, leaping over fallen logs and brambles alike until she found its resting place… but it was gone.

Scraps of brambles and leaves were scattered about and a trail in the loam led toward the water, as though something large had been dragged. Mei stopped at the river's edge with a sigh, bending at the bank to let her fingertips trail in the cool river. Was he heading for the Moon Gate and beyond? Could he even row? She hadn't noticed an oar. And how were his skinny arms going to haul the boat out of the water of a night?

"No. You'll use your power, just like I would," she whispered as she stood, shoulders slumping.

She dragged her feet a little on the way back.

On the one hand, she'd simply left without telling Siratta she was going, but on the other, her destination would have been obvious, if anyone had planned on seeking her out.

But once Mei reached the road, she quickened her stride. She had a lot of ground to cover if she was going to catch up to Iggy, and she didn't mean to let anyone stop her.

***

Mei hesitated near Arun's garden, glancing over the low stone wall to where the healer tilted his old watering can over fresh shoots, watching the liquid soak into dark earth. Every now and then, he paused to rest his hands upon the ground, growing still, as if waiting for something, perhaps.

But he moved with a stiffness she never really noticed at other times. Was he always hiding it? He *was* getting older.

"Mei?" Arun set his watering can down, peering up through the flowers.

"Arun, I…"

He smiled. "Sometimes all the wisdom in the world doesn't seem worth a young man's ease of movement, you know."

"I…" Still she hesitated, unsure of how to begin. "Were you seeking something in the earth?"

"Trying to find a trace of leylines, I suppose."

"Leylines?"

"Just something my grandfather once told me about; the earth's power. We should be able to feel them… but it is as though I have always been blocked." He shrugged as he moved around to sit on the low wall, then patted a space beside him. "Join me."

She did so. "Arun, I want to apologise… I'm sorry about before."

The Iemeda patted her hand. "I know. You were upset. Siratta has told you about Iggy?"

Mei nodded. "I don't know what to do. He still needs my help."

Arun scratched his head, sending pollen drifting down to settle on his shoulders. "Perhaps he doesn't, Mei." He paused, as if unsure of how to continue. "Have you considered that you need him more than he needs you?"

"Maybe." She gave a shrug. "But either way, I'm not going to abandon my brother."

Arun frowned. "You mean to follow him."

"Tomorrow morning."

"And where is he headed, and how will you follow?" Arun asked. "Have you thought this through?"

"I'm certain he's headed west, for the Moon Gate," Mei replied with a small nod. "He's using the river and a boat he made, letting it carry him downstream – I'm sure of that, since if he heads upstream, the village might seek him out. I'll follow on foot."

"Hmmm. Well, you are probably right about that. But your mother needs you here. I need you, we all do. What will the Inora do without one of their strongest minds, eh?"

Mei almost smiled. His words were the kind she'd been craving for a long time, but they were bittersweet now. Now, they were a little too late, even if they might have been the kind of words to make her stay. "Mother has Paragon Mikal. You have Ki to help you with your medicines. And the Inora survived for hundreds of years before I came along. I think it's the right decision."

Arun sighed. "Well, I doubt I can stop you. And I admit, there are dangers beyond the Moon Gate that your brother does not deserve to confront alone."

"Then you'll help me?"

He chuckled. "If I'm going to be co-conspirator in your flight, then I'd better do it properly. Give me a few moments."

Arun pushed himself up off the wall and walked to the house. When he returned, he was carrying two pouches – one blue and one an earthy red. "Now, take these with you when you go."

"Really?"

"Of course, dear."

She accepted his gift with an embrace, and when she pulled away, his eyes were wet. "Thank you, Arun. I know what these are worth."

"Just make it last," he said. "Have you decided what to tell the Paragons?"

She glanced away. "Nothing. I'm old enough to have my own husband; this summer will be my nineteenth. I've been an adult for nearly three years. The Paragons cannot stop me, not by custom and not by force."

"And Siratta?"

"She can tell them whatever she wants."

Arun rubbed at the stubble on his jaw. "Your father had your flair for pretending to misunderstand things too, as I remember. You know that's not what I'm asking."

"I do."

"Very well." He placed both hands on her shoulders. "Permit me one more time to ask you to stay. If not for my other reasons, then what if the Blood Cats are actually migrating north?"

It was a fair attempt, but her answer came easily; it was one that she had thought through on her walk back to the village as well. "Then we will be overrun with or without me, Iemeda. Only Ig could make a difference if that were true. Besides, Galarik will bring news, and if not, ask Seer Egril to do something useful for once." She spread her hands. "And couldn't the village move, if needed? It's been done before, right?"

"Not so easily, but you are correct," he replied with a deep sigh, and though his expression did not lighten very much, he still smiled. "Very well, then. May the Sun always shine upon you, Mei. Ig too."

"And you, Iemeda."

## CHAPTER 9. – ROKURA

Rokura cleaned and dressed Magdelai's wounds, taking an extra moment to brush leaves and dirt from her greying hair in the firelight. He was sweating from the nearness of the flames, but he'd needed the light. His pack had enough slug-rose for congealing and a little spirrom for the pain but judging her recovery was not so easy. The woman seemed too old to bear whatever forced march and other abuse she'd been put through.

There was every chance she bore other internal injuries he could not detect, let alone tend. But his efforts seemed to ease her pain, if not her worries.

Constantly she spoke of her grandson, Fara, taken with her from their small village farther west. From Magdelai's stories, he was able to plot part of the rebel's course across the Forest of Omaila, but their ultimate destination remained unconfirmed, as Magdelai could not understand Takirov.

But she was able to describe the leader.

"He is a gentle… brute of a man, My Lord."

Rokura frowned. "How so?"

"Sometimes, his impatience had him lashing out. At us or

his men, but never the children and never animals. He rescued a doe caught in brambles… it was strange."

"I see." A man of apparent contradictions. Yet that did not make him admirable. His trade was in people; no cause could justify such an act.

"I saw his eyes clearly," she said after a moment. "The sun shone down and before it set, they were waking us up to walk the night again. Fara agreed, looking into his eyes was like being swallowed." She shivered. "When he struck me, I scratched his cheek… but he only stared in response."

Rokura rested a hand on her shoulder. "Rest now."

"Thank you, My Lord."

"Will you be able to travel tomorrow, do you think?" he asked, accepting the cup she handed him and refilling it.

"So, we can follow them, I hope?" Her question was broken by a fit of coughing, and when she stopped, he saw blood on her lips.

Rokura kept a sigh of concern to himself. "Perhaps such a journey would be too much in your state, lady. I will take you to the nearest Wayside Inn but I mean to intercept them beyond the forest."

Her dark eyes burned in the firelight. "And you will rescue my boy?"

"I will do everything I can."

"Bless you, My Lord," she said, her eyes now closing in exhaustion. He stroked her hair a moment, eventually switching to a damp cloth to wipe her brow. "I will guard your sleep."

He turned his back to the light then and stared into the shadows, listening.

***

Magdelai did not survive the night.

Even in the weakness of the pre-dawn glow, a paleness to her face was apparent. Knowing no Common Prayers well, Rokura murmured a Call to the Idyll, his breath steaming in the coolness. As he arranged her limbs he paused. Dried blood lay beneath her fingernails. She had scratched the leader. *A sorcerer can use this.* Very carefully, he scraped the dried flakes of blood into a scrap of cloth with his knife.

Then, he wrapped her in the blankets and secured her body to his mount. "Forgive me, but you'll have to carry two today, my friend," he told Arrow. The roan stamped a foot and tossed his head.

Rokura broke camp quickly, then led Arrow from the hollow and to the road as the sun struggled through dark branches. There, he mounted up and started for the Wayside Inn; it lay between his camp and Cinder, and from there, it would be possible to contact Magdelai's village.

When he reached the small, two-storey inn with its thatched roof and spiralling vines of green and gold, the morning was not yet finished. No travellers on the highway and only a faint breeze twisting the small flag of blue that hung above the door – marked with twin vials that proclaimed the place was favourable to and favoured by the noble family of Miadu.

Which did not mean others would be turned away, only that Miadu received preferential treatment and a portion of the income.

*Ridiculous custom.*

He knocked on the wood and waited for the porter.

A short man bowed when he opened the door. "Welcome, My Lord. We are offering a noon meal in due time, if you have not eaten. Allow me to tend to your mount..." he trailed off.

"Water is sufficient," Rokura said. "As you can see, I have brought a woman who needs proper burial. I trust you can arrange that or to send word to her village, Daleis."

"My Lord." A flicker of interest passed over the man's face, but he did not question the Greyshield, instead moving directly to Arrow.

Rokura entered a sparse, clean common room. Its low ceiling was supported by a central column which doubled as a brick fireplace. The fire had been banked but not lit. At the bar waited a tall fellow, the innkeeper, and muffled voices drifted from the kitchen behind him and the rooms above too, as patrons readied themselves to eat or perhaps continue their journeys.

"How may I serve?" the owner asked with a bow.

"I need two pigeons, writing materials and water."

"Yes, My Lord. I will send for the water and return with the birds myself."

"You have my thanks." Rokura sat near the windows, one of only two travellers in the common room. The other traveller was an older woman, busy repairing a tear in her deep blue cloak.

A somewhat sleepy-looking boy soon brought water in a jug and Rokura accepted it with a nod. The lad waited while Rokura drank, but since he did not order food, the server excused himself with a deep bow.

The innkeeper returned almost on the boy's heels, carrying a quill, ink and small scrolls, standing back as Rokura composed his messages. One to the palace, informing the king of the rebels and their probable direction, and the second west to Ibetolo where Jonka would need to be informed.

Ibetolo was not so far from the rebels' path... but it was still a guess.

Rokura rolled up the messages with a small sigh. Then, he rose to follow the innkeeper upstairs and to a small room with a modest balcony where a black, cloth-covered cage waited. The pigeons stirred at the light, cooing to each other when the innkeeper removed the cloth.

"This must go to the palace." Rokura handed over the first message and the man tied it deftly to the foot of a pigeon, which had been taken from a perch marked 'Omaila.'

"And the second, My Lord?"

"Ibetolo."

The Innkeeper affixed the scroll to another bird then took both onto the balcony, where he cast them into the cool morning air. Rokura thanked the fellow with a pair of small coins. "The porter was tending to my mount; I will be leaving now."

"At once," the fellow replied, and hurried down toward the stable.

Once on the road again, Rokura left most of the navigating to Arrow's swift gallop, heading for the crossroads.

If Cinder the thief *was* telling the truth, and hadn't simply stumbled across the name of Asaro Itonye, then the slender fellow might hold vital information. Which meant that instead of needling a convicted man yesterday, perhaps taking him seriously had been the better option. Bringing him along on the hunt...

Perhaps no.

Either way, the thief's claim would now be investigated.

And even if Cinder proved to be a liar, then the column of rebels and prisoners could not travel fast. Catching them would be no problem, especially with their probable destination in mind. More, if gathering enough blades could be achieved, maybe interception and rescue were not out of the question.

Not in the least, he had promised Magdelai.

The sun was low in the sky when Rokura approached the crossroads where Cinder was living out his sentence. The man would be alive; it took longer than one day and night to die upon the cross.

Though how much of an object lesson such crossroad-deaths were had never been explained in a satisfactory manner. Travellers were usually quick to blot such sights out, to forget what they saw once they reached the beautiful garden city of Omaila. Its clean thoroughfares, shimmering architecture and sculpted gardens had that effect on people, who quickly lost themselves in the myriad wonders, and in certain quarters, vices.

Nor did the crucifixions seem to actually deter or reduce crime.

Lord Onga had once suggested affixing such displays to the walls, or even within the city itself, but that was no better – it was simply evil.

Yes, it would offend the delicate sensibilities of the nobility, setting up someone like Cinder on a cross in one of the Fine Markets and having the fops raise perfumed handkerchiefs to their noses, their waifish ladies wilting from horror… but the problem was the barbarism of the cross itself.

"Come back to taunt me, have you?" A shrill but rasping voice broke his reverie.

Cinder spoke from above, where he sagged against his bonds upon the cross. Blood had dried where the raven pecked him and his wrists and ankles were red and chafed from the bindings.

Rokura nudged Arrow closer, then stood in the stirrups, stretching to cut through the bonds one by one before wrapping an arm around the thief.

When the smaller man collapsed into his arms, it was to stare up at Rokura in a daze. "What is this?"

"Drink first," Rokura said as he dismounted, sitting Cinder against the post. Rokura went to his saddlebags next and returned with a flask. "A little at a time," he told the weakened man, who took the flask, only to upend it over his mouth.

Rokura snatched the flask back, sparkling water spilling forth. "Idiot," he growled as he returned the flask. "Slow down."

Cinder complied and Rokura gave him some time to appreciate his freedom.

"Now, Cinder the thief, here are my terms." He rested his foot on a stone beside the short fellow, drawing a dirk from his boot. "You will tell me what was in the letter and I will take you to whichever border my target is closest to."

The man's eyes sparkled with hope but he did not smile. "How do I know you won't just put me up there again once I talk? Your sense of justice and duty, remember?"

"You should know the Greyshields better than that. Once I make a promise, it will not be broken. And I'll make you two, right now, to help you decide. If you talk, I will take you to a border as requested." Rokura leant forward, until their noses were almost touching, and dropped his voice. "And if you betray me, I will drive this blade through your ear and into your skull – quite slowly."

Cinder swallowed, eyes darting from side to side. "I wouldn't like that, My Lord."

"I imagine not." Rokura hauled the man to his feet and dragged him to the horse. "Eat a little while you talk."

The thief moved on wobbling legs to the saddlebags and rummaged around a moment before drawing out some salted beef. He lifted it with a questioning look. Rokura nodded. Cinder took a few bites and then another drink before inhaling deeply.

"It's wonderful to be down from there." He wiped the sweat from his brow and shuddered. "Hard to believe, actually."

"Moving along."

"Well, as for the letter. It was from an unnamed party and addressed to someone named Bedoa. You recognise the name, I'm sure."

"Certainly." Duke Bedoa *was* the type to try his hand at treachery… if he were truly involved.

"In any event, the mark was rich and stupid. Rich because I found a little gold in his purse, and stupid because he'd kept the letter in the first place. But it had directions to the inn where he was to meet whoever wrote it, so I guess maybe he just has a poor memory."

"No need to describe his personal failings. Continue."

Cinder took another bite. "My interest was piqued, of course. A rich Nasaru meeting a stranger in a seedy Takirov tavern? Duke Bedoa obviously has money enough, what with the Black Coral and all, but my mark didn't look like a sorcerer stocking up on coral. The letter mentioned significant remuneration in exchange for specific maps of Nasaru, especially areas surrounding the capital."

Rokura nodded. "Go on."

Cinder shrugged as he took another big bite of the salted meat. "I wanted to know more, but that was when the extremely angry-looking guards burst into the inn. Of course, they collected everyone and during the course of subsequent questioning, I came under suspicion. Must have been the gold – one of them said I didn't dress 'Lordly' enough to carry such coin."

"Cinder, the facts are enough."

"Apologies, My Lord."

Rokura sighed. The rebels obviously wanted to avoid main roads and highways but equally likely, they wanted locations of villages. And they were targeting children and young men because they sought Asaro Itonye.

Bastard son of the king.

The perfect ransom.

Only, no-one knew exactly where the lad was hidden… supposedly. Had Bedoa learnt something? Tipped off the rebels for personal gain? Was the Duke actually involved at all? And above all, had Asaro Itonye already been captured? *Did I make a mistake? Asaro could have been mere yards away from me last night.*

Some stroke of fortune had let him cross paths with the thief… but had such fortune already been squandered? "Cinder, tell me what the letter said about Asaro Itonye."

"Only that he had to be located and taken to Takirov."

Rokura raised an eyebrow. "Someone actually wrote those

words down?"

"I saw them," Cinder said. "Why does that matter? Who is this Asaro Itonye, anyway?"

"Time to ride," Rokura said as he mounted Arrow, then reached down to yank the small man up after him. "Hold on." He snapped Arrow's reins and they leapt forward, cutting a parallel path with the rebels and their likely destination of the southern border.

"Where are we going?" Cinder shouted, his face pressed against Rokura's cloak.

"South toward the border – it is time for some hunting and tracking, ably assisted by you, of course."

"Assisted?"

"After which, you will be delivered as promised. I believe the Inora Valley is indeed the closest border."

## CHAPTER 10. – ROKURA

Rokura leant against Arrow's saddle and muttered curses to himself where he and Cinder rested beneath the boughs of a great pine, the almost sweet scent heavy upon the air. Despite his best efforts, after three days of tracking the rebels, their trail disappeared on the eastern side of Malkaha Marsh.

A green plain dotted with clumps of trees and patches of blade-grass stretched before him now. He glared in the hope of some sign, a whisper of smoke perhaps, *anything* to confirm the location of the Takirov and their prisoners.

It should have been painfully simple.

Twenty-odd people did significant damage to grass or goat trail, but either he had exited the forest at the wrong point, missing them by a mile for all he knew, or they were in possession of magic.

The rebels had crossed streams, concealed their camps and used occasional bouts of rocky terrain to cover their tracks prior. Once, Rokura found a broken buckle and even the frayed remains of a man's shirt, but in time, all hints of the rebels' passage vanished.

A troubling change in their behaviour, especially

considering the casual way they left Magdelai to die when he first found them.

*Past time I found some help.* It might have been a vestige of foolish pride that prevented him from asking earlier.

Rokura patted Arrow's neck even as he shook his head. A pipe and some leaf would have offered some calm, but he carried none. More, swearing off it only mattered if he kept his own promise to himself.

If nothing else, he would at least first keep his word to his travelling 'companion' if such a word could be used.

Rokura spoke over his shoulder. "Enjoy your freedom, Cinder."

The thief stood from where he lounged beneath the branches. "Ah, do you mean I'm finally on my own?"

He turned. "I do. Less than a day to the south-west you will find the Moon Gate, entrance to the Inora Valley."

The small fellow narrowed his eyes. "Hard to get into that Valley, I hear."

"Wait for a merchant."

"Even so, I doubt outsiders are welcome in Nokema."

Rokura shrugged. "Then go north and make for Cresideth. Or east to the coast, you might find a ship willing to take you. Or to sneak aboard."

"That is not a true choice, Greyshield," he said. "And a day's travel is *not* the border, as per your oath."

Rokura crossed the space between them, lowering his voice as he did. "Do you remember my other promise, Cinder?"

The man glanced away. "Fine."

"Yes, it is." Rokura returned to Arrow, then rummaged around in his pack. There he found a spare flask, which he tossed to the thief. "Find the River Inrik and follow it to the Gate." He mounted up then, not waiting for Cinder to respond, which the thief chose, quite wisely, not to do.

Cinder had served his purpose. In truth, Cinder's chatter no longer in his ear would be a blessed relief. If a little more generosity of spirit remained, Rokura could have admitted that he hoped the thief would actually appreciate how close he had come to death, and take good advice about the border.

Pragmatically, Cinder had provided a name – two names at that – and perhaps such revelations alone were worth whatever trouble the thief might cause others in the future.

***

Ibetolo's finest inn, the Stranger's Rest, did have a few creaking floorboards but its food was warm and well-seasoned, which certainly made up for any minor defects in the twin-storey building.

The Stranger's Rest was also crowded with men tired from a long day working the fields and all seemed to be enjoying their meals too. Petals dotted their tunics and sleeves, sometimes flying around the room when they spoke, arms waving in boisterous gestures. The fire spread warm light around the common room, though it barely touched Rokura.

His shadowy corner suited his mood.

Still no trace of the rebels. His promise to Magdelai weighed upon him. His promise to his fellows, his king and nation too. For what was a duty unfulfilled but a bitter stain upon his spirit? Whether the column had turned north, east or west wouldn't matter soon – not if a sorcerer could be found.

A serving girl approached, trepidation in her smile, but he ordered only more wine, not having the palate for a plate of sweetened plum drops traditionally offered after a meal in the southeast. And though the wine offered its own, subtler sweetness, rarely did he raise the glass to his lips. Its purpose was more to keep his hands busy while he waited. His messenger bird had already been and gone before his arrival. It meant the innkeeper met him with a message from Nata, a fellow Greyshield. It claimed she would be waiting for him at the Stranger's Rest but as yet she'd not appeared.

Rokura leant back in his chair when a figure in a grey cloak and hood entered, blade and bow visible. She glanced across the common room and started directly for the dim corner.

"Sitting alone, I see," Nata said as she approached, her melodious voice full of amusement. "Don't they like you here?"

He smiled. "Still not very punctual, I see."

Nata sat across from him, pushing her hood back to reveal long, dark curls. She laughed, dark eyes bright. "Ah, it's good to hear your grumpy voice again, Rokura."

"And you look well."

She'd changed in the two years since taking on her first post. Young to be a Greyshield, her face had a few lines but it was still a happy one, the kind any man could appreciate, but now her eyes were less trusting.

She had met the world and been altered by that meeting, it seemed... yet not for the worst. The last traces of any girlish hesitancy were gone; he saw a woman in the confident movements, in the cool way she kept an eye on the room, scanning exists and the faces within.

Before political scheming forced Rokura from Hyacinth Ridge, and rumours of the Takirov uprising kept him from returning, he had trained her – Nata was stern beneath her cheerful demeanour.

A wave of pride swept in but he tempered it with the truth; others had taken an equal role in training Nata, not in the least she herself.

"What does Mutolo have you doing here?" he asked, once a new serving girl had delivered more wine for Nata, the poor thing unable to quite meet their eyes. Her nerves shouldn't have been typical; after all, Greyshields were *protectors*... and yet, not every noble in the nation focused themselves upon noble pursuits. "Has Jonka been given a new post?"

"I saw you addressed your message to him," Nata said after taking a sip. "Apparently, the king thinks Jonka is getting too old. He's been recalled to the palace."

"Hmmm." Was that really the reason? "Jonka is barely ten years older than me."

She patted his hand. "Don't worry, I doubt you'll be next, if that's what you're thinking. You're old but not *that* old."

He scowled at her. "I could do without the jokes."

Nata chuckled. "Fine, fine."

"And I meant what I said in that letter – something is afoot," he continued. "The cipher?"

"I understood. You're right, it *is* serious but I haven't seen anything like that here and I've been watching for *anything*. Sometimes I think I'd rather be back at the Autumn Palace, babysitting Mutolo's sulking mother."

"Now, now, Nata," he said with a smile. "Queen Tiloba has a reputation as a cruel, cruel misanthrope; she can hardly be expected to smile all the time. Think what it would do to her cheeks – she could burst a blood vessel."

"Now who's being immature?" she said with a grin.

He raised his hands. "Point taken."

"So, are they no longer heading to Takirov, perhaps?"

"It would certainly add to the trouble they're already causing. I might not be able to catch them by now, but if I can at least confirm *where* they are headed, we can intercept them."

"How are things in the south?"

"You haven't heard?"

"Not if anything new has happened."

"Everything is still tense. The Takirov Sage and his Seedlings are denying any involvement in the violence, but who can say how far their sympathies go? Or their hatred."

"Is that entirely true?"

"Meaning?"

"The new Sage has been sending overtures of peace."

"Political posturing."

"Are you sure?"

He sighed. "You've been south, Nata. The hatred is certainly true of much of the populace. The fires, the beatings in the streets, how people of mixed-heritage there are treated. Our merchants no longer travel the northern parts of Takirov in safety, to say nothing of the Collectors."

"Can you blame them, Rokura?" She leant forward, lowering her voice. "Nasaru has hardly been an exemplary master all these centuries."

Rokura did not answer at once. "Perhaps. But insurgents running around whipping up frenzies in every small town from Gistle to Makiya do not make things easier. Tell me, is there a sorcerer in town?"

"Yes," she said after a pause of her own. "He's actually staying right here, which is why I suggested we meet at the Rest."

He stood. "Well then, the early bird catches the worm, right?"

# CHAPTER 11. – ROKURA

Rokura followed Nata to the sleeping quarters, slowing while she counted doors, most without any hint of light visible around the door jambs. She came to a halt in the middle of the corridor and knocked once.

"Yes?" The word drifted through the wood and it was somehow more precisely spoken than even the most prudish of his fellow lords back the palace.

"Is this the room of the Coral Sorcerer Eroya?"

"Yes, please come in."

Nata led Rokura into a wood-panelled room, dominated by a large desk. A cot had been crammed into a corner and the desk was covered in rows of vials and various shapes of sanded wood.

An older man bearing dark hair threaded with silver sat behind the desk, the jagged black patterns on his white robes gleaming in the candlelight – the sleeves especially had been stitched to represent the twisting Coral that lent sorcerers their power.

Eroya stood and moved around the desk to offer a bow. "My Lord and Lady. How may I assist you?" Again, the precision of his pronunciation was impressive, almost intense... as though... *words* mattered to the sorcerer, rather than the use of language being a status-marker?

"A simple matter, Sorcerer Eroya." Rokura drew the piece of cloth, careful not to let the dried blood flakes fall. "I wish to locate a man. I believe this is his blood."

Eroya let a whisper of a sigh free as he accepted the cloth. "That would be no trouble, My Lord." He returned to the desk where he removed a thin blade of tiny proportions and began scraping flakes of dark red into an empty vial. "However, I have a suggestion if I may?"

"Certainly."

"Should you wish to locate this man on separate occasions but *without* more of his blood, I could provide you with something more sophisticated than usual." Eroya lifted another vial, this with a clear liquid a little too thick to be water, adding it to the blood. Next came a liquid that was such a dark purple as to nearly be shadow – the Black Coral. "Admittedly, it is largely untested beyond the scope of blood, but I believe it will work across significant distances."

"We would appreciate that." Rokura felt a jab to the ribs. Nata looked to the sorcerer and then to the purse on Rokura's belt. "We will pay you today, of course," he added.

Nata was right to remind him. While Greyshields had every right to seek any service and have the king remunerate his citizens, the lengthy process was not one that merchants of any stripe looked forward to, let alone sorcerers.

"I appreciate the generosity. I will work quickly."

The three elements were beginning to combine, remaining dark but bearing a bright sheen. Rokura leant a little closer.

Rare to see the liquid in action. A thick, vibrant resin drained from Black Coral reefs in the southern ocean; it always seemed alive to Rokura, giving off a faint glow and a strange, cloying scent. No doubt the price of Coral had risen in the current unstable climate surrounding Takirov. It would be hurting sorcerers all across the lands, not just on the eastern coast.

"While fresh blood or hair or nail clippings would have worked perhaps better, there is enough here for the magic to function," Eroya explained as, from the table, he selected a wooden disc that fit easily into his palm. He poured the mixture onto the disc's surface and Rokura raised an eyebrow when it was absorbed. Other sorcerers would drink the potion and *then* perform the scrying themselves. With Black Coral being so poisonous to regular people, it was certainly a prudent way to conduct business – but by empowering an inanimate object, Eroya was reducing his own custom.

"I think you will find that this can show you the direction you need to travel in order to locate the man you seek." The sorcerer handed over the wooden disc.

Rokura nodded. The liquid had soaked through, the wood now dry, its only marking the hand-painted arrows set in the four directions. "Impressive."

Eroya bowed again. "Thank you, My Lord. It is something I have developed myself. This way, even non-sorcerers can use magic, though I am having less success with other materials. Glass and crystal simply do not hold the Coral."

"How does it work?" Nata asked.

"Simply face any direction. Even if that choice is wrong, the correct arrow will emit a faint glow to show you the way."

Rokura turned north and the southern point began to glow

faintly purple.

"I will also complete a more traditional search if you wish?" Eroya offered.

"This will be more than enough," Rokura replied. He removed three silver marks from his purse. "If you also wished to send a claim to the city, I'm sure Nata would be willing to sign Note of Service."

"Oh..."

"It's fine," Nata said with a smile. "You've earned something extra."

***

The next day at dawn, Rokura returned Nata's wave from the edge of Ibetolo. Her grey cloak and hood blended with the morning mist, a pale glow from the nearest home clinging to the foggy air.

It was a chill morning for spring, and the cloudy sky hinted at rain. Rokura pressed his lips together. The weather wouldn't make any difference to the wooden disc he'd been given but it would further dampen his mood.

Arrow led him south and together they followed the faint glow on the disc, the sound of hooves muted in the hush as Rokura scoured the green plains for signs of his quarry.

And not until noon did an ache in his stomach draw him to a halt long enough to eat beneath the noon sun, a pause for which Arrow seemed equally grateful. "Sorry, boy," he said, patting the horse's neck.

When Rokura mounted up and rode on once more, the afternoon was not yet half over before he found himself reining in again, this time at a low mound.

Some distance from a stand of trees, the mound was a

conspicuous patch of earth, set as it was in a slight depression and surrounded by gently swaying grass. And it lay directly upon the path the rebels had taken – at least, according to the sorcerer's disc.

Rokura dismounted and knelt to run a hand over the mound. Not old at all; grass had yet to break through at the edges of the soil and it was easy to penetrate the top layer with only the pressure of his fingers.

That the rebels bothered to bury a body suggested some concern over their tracks, out in the comparative open of the plain. While any fool would notice that a large amount of people had passed this way, a bound body lying in the grass would certainly give an unwanted clue as to that group's purpose.

*Assuming this has anything to do with my quarry at all.*

Rokura rose to scout the area, and soon found a trail of trampled earth, some of the weeds half-risen now. The path continued south, drifting around toward the coast. He drove his fist into his palm, a rush surging through his limbs. *You won't be able to compete with Arrow.*

But he did not leave at once – he owed it to Magdelai to at least check the grave for her grandson, Fara.

Brushing aside a layer of topsoil, Rokura soon switched to a sheathed dagger, making steady progress. Soon, he had scooped enough earth to uncover a leg. He paused to press his lips together. The skin was white and bruised.

Someone from afar, then.

Poor little one.

He kept working, uncovering torso and arms next. The corpse was quite thin, dressed in a ragged collection of clothing uncommon to Nasaru. The cross stitching of two colours seemed familiar, but not Takirov. "I'm sorry for what happened to you," he said, voice hushed. Uncovering more of the slender body, Rokura reached the throat and finally uncovered the head.

A strangled gasp escaped his mouth and he fell back, hands shaking.

The boy had no face.

## CHAPTER 12. – MEI

Mei knelt by the grassy banks of the Inrik and its steady flow, leaves and dark needles swirling around the nearest bend. She tossed a smooth stone into the water and received only a muted splash as her reward. Had Iggy really passed the same way, mere days ago?

He could leave the river at any point, especially beyond the Gate, but he wouldn't be in a rush to do so. He needed to stay close to water.

For now, she *was* still on the right path… hopefully.

She straightened to stare down at the sleeping village in the featureless dawn light. Maybe for the last time. *Nokema.* 'Circle by the River' the first Paragons had named it, well over two hundred years ago when hundreds of her people were left stranded by the War of Tombs.

And now she was leaving.

Yet taking another step… her limbs didn't seem to want to respond.

It wasn't just turning from the few people she truly trusted but leaving an *entire* life. *Everything I know. Our homes, our food… the sound of our voices.* The world beyond did not know or understand the gifts of the Inora either. It would be lonely. And dangerous.

At least, so the Paragons always claimed.

But the stories about the wars, about the vicious, untrustworthy Nasaru and their enormous, dark cities… they were exaggerated, surely. The past was gone. Today, wouldn't the Nasaru peoples be more like Denuko Gree?

*Or is that just wishful thinking?*

Either way, once she trod the unknown earth beyond the Moon Gate, she would need to hide her identity to be safe. Because if even half of what the Paragons claimed was true, then the Nasaru were likely going to be suspicious at best.

Once, several Inora settlements existed in the plentiful valley hidden within the Dalma Mountains, but over time, the Inora had been forced together. Arun claimed that what drove them to the site of Nokema was mostly the Blood Cats, unfavourable weather, and the change of a river course.

To hear Paragon Mikal describe the reason it was deep, painful memories of times before the Moon Gate was discovered; times when Nasaru attacks were common, since they not only feared the Inora gift, but mistook inhabitants of the valley for their old enemies – the Senoja peoples.

Since then, none but the most hardy lived beyond the protective circle of Nokema by choice. Those who were banished were rumoured to live west, deep in the Giraj or 'Glass' Forest.

But if Iggy was going to search those people out, some said to be as powerful as they were unstable, Mei would follow. If he was going farther, if he was going *Beyond* – going through the Moon Gate to the lands of the supposedly warlike Nasaru

– then she would follow him there too.

"Time to go." Mei took another step at last, continuing up the fishing trail where it ran by the river, heading west toward the edge of Nokema.

She did not glance back.

Was it guilt? No… Perhaps there was only one thing being left behind, and it was her absence. No-one else had been afforded a goodbye, not even Siratta. So, too, would Mei leave behind the absence of her pack, blanket and travel rations taken from the pantry, a small pot and also her father's antique blade, included almost as an afterthought.

*Be honest. You snuck it from a drawer in Siratta's room, like a thief.*

No-one in the village carried such a weapon.

Knives used for daily tasks were simpler, shorter affairs and Father's dagger was almost the length of Mei's forearm, inlaid with a series of interlocking lines. The pale blade even bore a small, circular hole near the hilt – a deliberate choice based on the way the lines were arranged.

Hard to even guess at its value in the outside world.

But its weight was unpleasant where she'd affixed a sheath to her leather belt. Even the thought of touching such a weapon… All her life, the village preached the evils of war and its sharp tools. Mei ran a fingertip across a faint scar upon her forefinger – a stinging gift from her curiosity as a child.

Then, when Siratta had found her clutching a bleeding finger, she bandaged Mei up and told the story of the knife. "It was passed down in your father's family from the days of the First Wars, long, long before we came to the valley or Nokema and gave up such weapons. Did you know your father would joke that it once belonged to a sun-killer his grandfather fell in love with?" Siratta had shrugged. "But who knows? Either way, I hope you realise how dangerous this is now."

As Mei walked, heavy pack weighing upon her still-healing shoulder, she scanned the trail ahead. For the most part, there were only trees and grass beside the river… except that wasn't true.

Mei slowed when a figure detached itself from a boulder.

It stopped in the centre of the path.

Someone come to say goodbye? To ask her to stay? *No.* Mei slowed even further as she neared. A woman dressed in a familiar pale robe. Aunt Wifral.

Mei stopped.

"So, you're sneaking away like a rat in the dark?" Wifral's arms were folded. The woman's broad features were twisted into an ugly mask of grief and hatred, the dawn light casting her eyes in shadow.

"No," Mei said, but her voice was not so steady. Guilt could not be denied. "I'm not sneaking away at all."

Wifral moved closer, and she was breathing hard. "Then what are you doing, *niece?*"

"Leaving. To find Iggy."

But it was obvious Aunt Wifral already knew why – and also that she did not approve at all. Her shoulders trembled. Spittle was clear upon her mouth, coloured with dark spots. Blood?

"Aunty?"

Wifral advanced and the air grew still.

Deathly still.

Mei tensed but too slow – an unseen blow to the stomach drove her to one knee. A stunning flash followed. It was so bright that her senses failed – and for just a moment, Mei was cut adrift, no idea whether she had hit the ground or not, whether it was day or night. Worse, her own psychic powers were equally impossible to reach.

Something crashed atop her, hands clawing at her throat.

Mei kicked out but Wifral's rage was too great, and it seemed her aunt brushed aside each blow like a feather.

Black rings filled Mei's vision as iron-like fingers dug into her skin. She gasped for air as she thrashed, continuing to beat at Wifral's face and shoulders, but the woman did not react. Mei's very body screamed for air. She fumbled at the ground for a stick or a rock, anything to use as a weapon, anything to give relief, but found nothing.

She was going to die.

Her fingers brushed against the handle of her father's dagger.

Darkness was rushing in.

Mei swung the blade with her remaining strength. The edge hit and sliced through something soft. Warm blood splashed across Mei's cheeks. She flinched, even as a piercing shriek echoed.

The crushing grip on her throat had vanished, the weight upon her body too. Sweet, sweet air rushed painfully down Mei's throat, filling her lungs. She rolled onto her side, gasping, blinking away tears. The grassy scent of earth was close now, her other senses returning quickly; her gift, too.

Wifral was close, but the force of her rage was fading, replaced by... shock and panic?

Climbing to her knees, Mei turned her head. Wifral knelt nearby, moaning into her hands, blood spilling between her fingers.

Mei's stomach heaved.

Hot liquid splashed onto the grass between her hands and she shuddered, coughing and spitting the remnants of her breakfast. She rose and stumbled away from the vomit, wincing at the acid on her tongue but just as much, at the surge of pain from her act of violence.

Or her fear at being attacked once more?

But Wifral hadn't followed. Instead, she was pawing at her face – eyes wild, voice rising, blood everywhere. A huge flap of skin that used to be the woman's cheek revealed red tendons. Even her nose was only half-connected now, the antique blade having cut deep.

"No." Mei stumbled back farther, the weight of the pack almost welcome as it drew her away.

Wifral shouted from behind her hands. "Is it not enough to kill my daughter?"

Mei fled.

## CHAPTER 13. – MEI

Mei was still stumbling on by noon, feet barely lifting enough to clear small stones on the trail, but somehow moving forward. Stubbornly, if nothing else.

Aunt Wifral had not followed.

Was the woman still alive? She'd be seeking help at home, surely. Mei had nearly stopped to cast the blade aside at one point, but even standing, arm raised above the river's shimmering surface, she could not let the dagger go.

What other links to Father were left?

And where she was going, she might need it for protection – her Inora abilities were not infinite. More, there was no longer a home for her in Nokema, it seemed. Not anymore. Which meant changing in order to survive in the outside world. Especially when it came to protecting Iggy. *But it'll take more than violence to help him.*

Her arms were trembling. So much was still unknown. Everything before her seemed so, so vast. *I'm just a young woman from an isolated village. I don't know anything.*

Despite the rumbling from her stomach, Mei had not stopped to eat. The sunlight was enough for now, offering strength. And even a little comfort.

Now she plodded on with the trail as it drifted away from the Inrik. The path still ran parallel with the water as moved into green hills that seemed almost too bright beneath the clear sky. Most were mere bumps in a grassy landscape, cut clear through by the broadening trail. It was fast becoming an old road of half-buried stone, once fully paved, no doubt. An unimportant fact, but she kept walking without pausing to examine the worn stone markers or the wagon ruts.

Walking was too important.

*Keep walking.*

It didn't really quell the doubts, but it was better than staying still.

Mei exhaled when she finally did pause, sitting upon a road marker and staring ahead. A faint blue waited in the distance where the Glass Forest rose. It stood cool and tall, familiar and seemingly welcoming. She would probably reach it by nightfall, even at her uneven pace, and find shelter before the darkness came to weaken her.

On any other journey, excitement at the thought of the reflective blossoms inside might have stirred in her chest but there was nothing much inside now; a numbness left behind after the guilt, horror, and exhaustion had worn away.

*I could rest here. For just a moment.*

She yawned and slid down to lean against the warm stone...

***

"Are you all right, girl?" An accented voice drifted into Mei's consciousness. "Is that Mei from Nokema Village?"

She woke with a jolt.

A shadowy figure on a wagon sat outlined against the

darkening, lavender sky, shadows falling across the hills.

Her eyes adjusted as she straightened.

An older man with a kind smile leant down from his seat, one of his horses flicking its ears. Dressed in a faded brown cloak that concealed his Merchant's Collar and its numbers, he held the reins in large, dark hands and peered down at her from under a wide-brimmed hat.

"Mei, what are you doing out here alone?" He climbed from the seat to kneel before her. "Do you need help?"

"Denuko Gree," she finally blurted out.

Up close, the Nasaru man's brown hair peeked from beneath the hat and the small scar on his clean-shaven chin was clear, even in the failing light. It was a scar he told everyone he won fighting off bandits – something he later revealed to her in secret to be a scar actually received in a fall from his wagon seat.

He smiled again. "Of course. Who else?"

"You're a bit late," she said, her surprise robbing her of anything intelligent to say.

Denuko chuckled. "That I am."

He helped Mei to her feet, leading her to the painted wagon and there they leant against its yellow wheels. He rummaged through a pack. "You know, the road is never the same. There are new twists and turns every year."

She accepted a flask of water he handed her and took a long drink, though she could have used her own.

"Is anything amiss in Nokema?"

"Yes. I…yes," she said, unsure of where to begin. "You can tell?"

He nodded. "Even someone simple as me could guess. You, so far from the village, alone and sleeping against a guide stone. It's not what I expect whenever I come here."

"Well…" Mei could not find words at first. "Iggy was Banished but he ran away and I'm following him." Tears threatened as the rest tumbled after. "Blood Cats attacked Nokema and Hishi was killed and it was all my fault! I wasn't strong enough to save her, Denuko. And Siratta is happy he's gone, Ig told her he *wanted* to leave. He built a boat and went downstream days ago and I think he's going through the Gate but I'm going to help him. I just have to catch up but I can't stop worrying – he could be Beyond by now already, and there's more," she said, taking a breath. "Aunt Wifral –"

"Slowly, Mei." The merchant raised one of his large hands, an expression of concern on his face. "Take another drink. And maybe another breath or two while you're at it."

Mei did so, then sighed. "Thank you."

"Mei, this is serious. For you and for Iggy. When the river becomes the Curajithcan farther downstream, it can be swift and dangerous. How will you catch him and how will you survive the Beyond when you do?"

"I just have to find him first."

"Hmmm. And you say he went by boat?"

"Maybe four days ago."

"Then he could be Beyond already." Denuko removed his hat and ran a hand through his hair before replacing it. "A boy without a face in Nasaru? He's not ready for that. You're right to follow him but *you* might not be ready either."

"I am." Mei focused her gift on his hat, plucking it from his head to send it spinning through the air. It came to rest on a dark tree stump, on the other side of the road.

"Very funny, young lady," he said as he strode after the hat.

"It's not meant to be, Denuko." She followed him across the road. "Could you have stopped me doing that?"

"Not the way you mean, no. But not all dangers come from the mind."

She pressed her lips together, and her shoulders slumped. *He's right, of course.* "I know. I'm sorry, I am. But I've made up my mind. Can't you help me?"

Denuko bent to retrieve his hat. "If I don't, who will?"

"Thank you."

The merchant smiled. "And I think I'll start by making camp and doing a bit of cooking."

***

After a welcome meal of chicken spiced with something quite peppery, Mei found herself too weary for much else. She prepared her bedding between stores on the wagon that Denuko rearranged for her. They were items he'd brought to trade with the Inora, the crates and barrels like little walls that left a square of stars visible overhead.

The merchant lay wrapped in his own blanket beneath the wagon, retiring after setting wards around his camp. Mei didn't know what the heavy steel poles were for, but Denuko believed in them, so trusting the mysterious things seemed like the right thing to do.

The Blood Cats hardly strayed so far north, either. Her safety probably wasn't in question. And yet, she couldn't sleep. "Denuko?"

Nothing.

She raised her voice to call again. "Denuko, are you awake?"

"Not anymore."

"Sorry. But are you sure those things work? There's no line

or bells or anything between them."

"I know. It's old Cresideth magic. If anything tries to pass into the camp, the poles will resonate and trap the intruder."

"Resonate?"

"Yes. The sound will wake us too, but I don't think it's ever happened this close to Nokema."

"Not once?"

He seemed to be shifting, rolling over perhaps. "Not in my memory."

"So, it's Cresideth magic?" It was such a far away land. Could it truly be so wondrous to create such things? *Maybe one day, somehow, I'll be able to see for myself? After I find Iggy.*

"Something like that."

"Oh."

"Don't forget, you're one of the strongest of the Inora – not many things out there to trouble you, you know," he said, and it sounded as though he smiled.

"I guess so." And yet Aunt Wifral's attack had been enough to cut off her power. *Is that something I should know how to do? I think I can remember what she did… maybe.* How did the woman fare now? Had she made it back to the village? Mei turned from the sky, as if the stars could see her shameful secret.

"If you like, I'll stay awake until you drift off," Denuko said.

Mei hesitated. Was it a little pathetic, a grown woman needing someone to watch over her? But when she answered him, it wasn't at all to say that such a thing would be unnecessary.

CHAPTER 14. – MEI

"Ready?" the merchant asked where they stood next to his horses, Flip and Saffron, the rising sun warm upon her back.

"I am," she said. "Thank you again."

Denuko had added to her meagre supplies, offering dried fruits and meat, a single silver coin and a warning. "You'll need that and more. Few people barter the way you Inora do."

She turned the coin over in her fingers, marvelling at the way it caught the light – since holding money was something she'd done only a few times in the past. A falcon wearing a crown had been stamped onto its surface, with enough detail to suggest two shades to the feathers. "I remember the first time you told me about money. Paragon Mikal was furious," she said with a laugh.

Denuko smiled. "The poor chap was, wasn't he? Well, that silver crown is worth at least three simple meals in the southern inns of Nasaru." He paused. "I'm not sure drwhat your story should be, Mei."

"I'm looking for Ig; that's my story. You don't think the truth will be enough?"

"Any soldier worth their salt will pick you up as a spy the

moment they lay eyes on you."

She frowned. "Do we Inora really seem that way?"

Denuko loosened his cloak, revealing the merchant's collar with its symbols of scales, including the sturdy-looking Nasaru numbers. "Remember this?"

"I do."

"Well, the War of Tombs changed a lot of things in the outside world, and not just for we merchants, if you'll remember."

"I do." He meant the way the two nations now had so little trust, something Mikal often mentioned too. How all travellers, not just merchants, were suspected and how the Nasaru Kings spent so much time building up their armies.

"Good. Then more importantly for you, while the nations of Senoja and Nasaru are constantly accusing each other of sending spies across the border, tensions are higher than usual. And yes, you look enough like your ancestors in the west that you will draw the wrong attention sooner enough."

"So the Paragons have always said, but we Inora left hundreds of years ago. We don't even –"

"You and I know that, Mei," he interrupted with a sigh. "But regular people in Nasaru will probably see you as Senoja. Most don't even realise that a place like Nokema still exists. But the similarities are clear, you know."

"Oh?"

"Same fair hair and pale skin; you could pass for a Senoja princess, Mei."

She stared at the ground.

Finding Iggy had been about as far as she'd thought things through. Ridiculous, really. A thousand dangers awaited and she knew nothing of most of them. Passing through the

Valley and finally the Moon Gate, catching Iggy, they were all problems enough; she hadn't bothered to consider *exactly* what lay ahead.

And being mistaken a spy from a land she had never set foot in, let alone *seen*, that just didn't seem fair.

Mei straightened. "If they'd imprison someone like me, what will they do to Ig?"

"I don't know," Denuko replied. He removed his hat again to scratch at his head. "Perhaps nothing, if Iggy really has become as strong as you say."

"Then I have to find him before then." *Before he lashes out, too.*

"I truly hope that you can, Mei."

"Well, if I need a story after all, what should it be?"

He smiled. "You might be able to pose as a healer, considering you have some knowledge."

"How?"

"Well, here and there, healers who were once imprisoned during border disputes are working in Nasaru. The last flare-up was only… five years ago, I'd say, and not all of them returned home, so you might be able to pose as one. Think you could manage that?"

Mei nodded. Finally, some luck! "I'm not as good as Ki but I think so," she replied. "But I didn't know there were still Senoja people in Nasaru."

"Not so many that you'd notice every place you went, but healers especially can be quite dedicated."

"But wouldn't they miss their homes? Their families?"

"I would expect so," he replied. "Yet some settled in Nasaru and started families of their own."

"I see." She frowned. "Then, does that mean that everyone

suspects them, too?"

Denuko sighed. "Plenty of people, yes. But healers are still incredibly important people. Which is why I believe you should pretend to be one. In fact, there is a special group of travelling healers that might be very helpful; the Fiodan."

"So, I would pretend to be one?"

"Hmmm. It would be easier to be yourself and seek their aid, instead. If you came across them, you would recognise the distinctive staff they carry, since it's carved to appear as though it has been entwined by a serpent."

"Then I'll do my best to convince people I am a healer."

"Good," Denuko said, patting her shoulder before climbing into the seat of his wagon and gathering the reins. "Now, I'd best be off. But if your search leads you so far as a large town called Solambe, seek a man named Walking Walter. He is a friend of mine and will help you if you mention my name."

"Walking Walter?"

He chuckled as he snapped the reins and Flip began to draw the wagon away. "Ask him to explain the name."

"Thank you, Denuko," she called after him.

Denuko lifted his hat to wave, and she watched the merchant and his wagon until they grew small, finally swallowed up by the road.

And then she was alone again.

*Get used to it – you have to depend on yourself.* Mei nodded in response to her own admonishing, letting rays from the sun continue to sink into her body a little longer, then spun and started toward the pale line of the Glass Forest at a jog.

A niggling doubt followed. It was too late to ask Denuko to keep her whereabouts secret. Would anyone set out after her? Wifral might have already returned... it probably didn't matter. And if so, nothing Denuko could offer, even if she ran after and asked, would make any difference. For better or worse.

***

Mei paused at the edge of the forest, stepping into the shade to listen and seek for anything amiss, using both her eyes and her mind.

An old wood, the Glass Forest bore pale blue and green leaves and smooth bark – deceptively soft to the touch. In the right light, a whole tree appeared as a shadowy mix of the two colours. Even the sparse undergrowth was subdued. No wildflowers grew, but vines with tiny purple blossoms squeezed between broad, flat rocks beneath the towering trunks of the trees, their dense canopies blocking much of the life-giving sunlight. Placing her hand upon the bark of one, she marvelled at the even surface.

But it was the reflective glass blossoms of the Pilor tree that were most spectacular – high above, and sometimes lying cracked on the ground, were its pale flowers, shining like glass.

Only they were not, of course.

But they were always warm, as though, like the Inora, they were drawing in the sun's warmth. "Which, I suppose they are," she said when she lifted one, then placed it into her pack with a small shrug.

Mei headed deeper into the woods, drifting from the path a few times to harvest some of the bitter molxa herb and sweet rasij with her belt knife. Best to have a range of supplies on hand for her ploy when she ventured Beyond.

If Iggy had already gone so far...

While her path took her from the Inrik's banks, the road and the river had the same destination – the Moon Gate. Not being able to check the oft-inaccessible river for signs of his passage was troubling, but hurrying to the Gate was far better than slogging her way through inaccessible terrain.

Dappled light grew brighter as she neared a clearing and in the branches overhead, tree-mice chattered away as they gathered seeds. Mei smiled as she travelled, ignoring the rumblings in her stomach a little longer, just enough to reach the clearing. There, according to memory, if she veered off the path a little way, a fallen log greyed with age would be a suitable sun-bathing location.

*So long as I'm actually remembering this part of the forest properly.*

When she reached and then circled the clearing, coming across the trail, she found the old log with a smile. "Perfect." She climbed atop and stretched out for the sun with a sigh. Had Iggy found similar places? How did he fare each night? He couldn't really stray far from the river, whatever his choices.

Once, he'd lasted several days without water but there had been a cost.

Mei chewed on an apple as she let the sun do its work. She would have to fill her own flasks again soon, too. In the meantime, she had what Denuko gave her. And the river and connected streams weren't far – off in the distance to the right, where the Inrik swung back around to head for the Moon Gate.

A two-day journey through woods that the Inora generally distrusted but would visit if needed, was now all that stood between Mei and her goal.

The Glass Forest *could* be passed, safely for the most part, not in the least because traders like Denuko Gree had been visiting Nokema since before she was born. But that didn't mean the place was free from dangers. Exiled Inora lived in the Glass Forest, and supposedly strange creatures dwelt in its dark centre, guarding vile hatchlings and snaring those foolish enough to wander into their hunting grounds.

Denuko had scoffed at these stories, assuring her she'd come to no harm so long as she kept to the road. "Once, I thought I caught a glimpse of a figure hiding in the trees by the old bridge, but it was most likely a deer or other animal, I'm betting. In all my years travelling this road, I have never seen a dark creature, nor encountered any of the Inora living in the woods, for that matter."

The supposed threats didn't really match her memories of the place, either. The Glass Forest had been wondrous when she'd visited in the past. Mei finished the last bite of her apple before climbing down to resume her search.

It wasn't likely she'd gain much ground on Iggy until she reached the Moon Gate, where he would most likely pause to gather strength. There was perhaps a small chance he would still be resting even now, but where would he go once he'd passed through? Would he leave some sort of trail?

To have any chance of sensing his power, she had to be a *lot* closer. And Nasaru was a nation many, many times larger than the Valley. In fact, according to Denuko, half the Valley could be contained inside Nasaru Lake in the far north. And though she listened closely to his tale, the idea of a lake so vast... he had been exaggerating, surely.

By the time evening brought its cool shadows, Mei had already found a campsite.

A relatively flat piece of ground in a tiny clearing offered room for her blankets. The soft but tall trunks of the Pilor trees provided shelter, along with kindling for a fire. She created a steeple of twigs and frowned down at the flint and steel as she worked until the sparks set bone-dry moss she'd gathered aflame.

Next, she boiled water for tea in her small pot, chewing on the salted meat from Denuko before finishing her meal and lying back in the hush. Once again, her muscles ached from walking all day, and the darkness didn't allow for a swift restoration, but sleep was still vital.

She rolled onto her good shoulder, staring into the dark.

The Glass Forest might have been a little too quiet compared to home but the closeness of the trees was not like being exposed on the open road. Instead, the trunks rose like dark sentinels, their shadows cloaking her. Somewhere, hopefully not too far distant, Iggy would be feeling just as secure... so long as he wasn't having nightmares.

Or maybe he was already far Beyond, somewhere in Nasaru? *Iggy, I hope you're safe.*

Sleep did not come swiftly.

## CHAPTER 15. – MEI

Birdsong roused Mei. She pushed the blanket aside to stretch her limbs and brush a tangle of blonde hair from her face. The morning was warm and sunlight already a little too high between the leaves, gleaming on the glass blossoms. She'd overslept, dogged by unpleasant dreams that drifted free of her grasp as she stood.

Had they been about Iggy? Her aunt?

Mei wolfed down some of the dried fruit as she snatched up her belongings, then stomped her way into her boots to strike out for the road without a backward glance.

She had not been travelling long before coming across a fallen tree.

The trunk and its shattered branches, leaves splayed across the ground, might have blocked the trail if someone hadn't hacked and then sawed through. They'd rolled aside a portion of the tree, leaving enough space for a wagon. Mei smiled. Twists and turns indeed.

She hesitated between the halves, reaching out to run her fingers over the rough edges of the rings visible inside the trunk. Evidence of the Guardians at work, their grave desire to tend to what the Gods had seen fit to create... and abandon.

No time to linger.

The fallen tree was not so far behind when she came to the bridge known as First Bridge. It was a modest stone span, crossing the Inrik where the river naturally narrowed, and seemed a thing of permanence. Dark moss, a blue very close to black, clung to the underside of the bridge and the carvings on its sides were worn from wind and rain.

The shapes were unclear. It had long been a matter of good-natured argument in Nokema as to exactly what they had been, with some certain the carvings had been Circles of the Sun, evidence of Inora craftsmanship. Others thought the carvings belonged to whomever roamed the Valley in the centuries before.

A still pool waited beside the road on the far side, most likely fed from the river, and it was so clear that minerals sparkled within the stony bottom. Mei knelt beside it to refill her flask.

Wifral's bleeding face lay within the water.

Mei flinched back, flask rolling away.

*What was that?*

When she leant over again, the surface was clear. She exhaled with a shudder, waiting for her aunt to rise, water and condemnation pouring from Wifral's eyes and mouth...

But nothing.

"I won't stop," she said through gritted teeth, then retrieved her water flask and plunged it into the pool. Bubbles roared up, and she refilled the flask, then stood with a grunt, setting off again.

Mere days since the attack and of course memories haunted

her. If hallucinations were the cost of what she'd done, then so be it. "I can bear that burden," Mei muttered. "I have to."

So long as finding Iggy was part of the bargain.

Mei moved into a jog. It was not quite noon, so reaching the edge of the woods where it encountered the Dalma Mountains and the Moon Gate by nightfall was still possible, even with a late start. At least, that's how it seemed during her last visit – years ago now, for the Rite of Caution. During the Rite, a triad of families would visit various places, including the Gate, to show children where it lay and explain why it existed.

The road wound on between the rows of pale tree trunks, and for the first time since entering the forest, she came across side trails. Some were of equal width to the main road but she followed the occasional wagon ruts, those heading ever-northward toward the Gate.

By late afternoon, Mei was growing weary once more. A decent clearing to sunbathe would help, but as her gaze roved across the forest, it fell upon an old signpost that stood before a fork in the road, not unlike a serpent's tongue.

Not so ancient as the bridge, the sign had been repaired several times, considering the difference in lichen and timber. Sharp symbols that were empty of meaning marked both the left and right trail. Denuko could have read them.

Both paths seemed similar enough and both continued north. And whether they swung around at one point or not, the choice was easy – left, since it followed the river and the river would pass through the Moon Gate.

Decision made, Mei adjusted her pack upon her shoulders and strode forward. Better to cover as much ground as possible before the forest swallowed up the last of the light.

And light between the tree trunks *did* grow thinner the farther she travelled. The pines and glass trees were older here, standing together too close, as if jostling and competing for the sunlight above. The rocks and vines below sat covered with more dark moss, and a dampness seemed to spread from the murmuring river.

Aside from the Inrik and her footfalls, the Glass Forest had grown quiet. No birds or small animals here.

Mei shivered as somewhere beyond the leaves, the sun set.

As Inora, each evening when rays from the sun slipped beyond the horizon, even without seeing the exact moment, a chill came. It meant relying on sleep, food or sometimes even medicine for sustenance – like people in other nations. And it worked just fine; but there was always something *more* when it came to the sun.

Especially for her Inora gifts.

But a peculiar light did remain.

Opposite the river, a pale flicker moved between the trees. Low to the ground, it remained stationary for brief moments only before continuing on a little farther and then coming to a halt.

Another traveller, perhaps. Mei tensed. Or one of the Inora, sent into Exile of the Valley. Someone or something else? So few outsiders sought out the Valley to begin with. Mei took a slow step forward. Setting up a camp of her own as best she could in the darkening wood was an obvious option, but what if the other person was dangerous somehow?

*I have to be sure – I don't want them to see my fire.*

Mei crept after the light, threading her way through the

trunks, sometimes having to squeeze between the soft bark of the Pilor. But steadily enough, she neared the glow without sounding like a rampaging boar.

And yet, the light didn't seem to be growing any closer.

She rubbed her eyes, then looked back. The road and the river were not visible or even audible now, and she'd taken at least a hundred steps. The glow shouldn't be so distant still. A trick of the wood? She tried to approach from a new angle, but again, made little progress.

"Guardians help me," she muttered, and increased her pace as best she could, using her mind to sense shrubs, roots and stones, but no matter how swiftly she navigated the falling dark, she could not close with the shining light.

"So be it." Mei swallowed a curse as she quickened her pace and leapt over yet another tangle of roots – only to crash into a branch with an echoing crack.

The light winked out.

A chill ran through her limbs as she rose, rubbing her shoulder. "Damn it." She leant against the bark of the nearest tree. The cold of the wood pressed against her skin, penetrating even her cloak and tunic as she listened, ignoring the dull throb of pain.

Long moments passed with only her breathing audible.

A twig snapped.

Mei flinched, scrambling away. What was there? Shadows loomed as she flitted through the trees, totally reliant on her mind now. Her feet skimmed over loam and stone alike, hands brushing aside shrubs and sometimes even pulling her along as she clutched at branches.

It was only possible to move so well now that her other

senses were no longer taking the lead, but how long could she keep it up?

Another sound – this time to her right.

Who was it? Who was out there, chasing her?

She flinched left, pivoting around a hole in the ground. It had been left by a fallen tree and the exposed roots scratched her cheek as she passed. The flash of pain was dull compared to her rising panic. Was it the owner of the light, charging between the trees in the dark?

It had to be one of the Inora to keep up. A bitter Exile?

Mei ran harder, dodging now like a ghost; nothing could touch her, no branch, leaf or rock, she was nearly flying! Ahead, a new light, nothing like before – the pale smudges of a clearing? Perfect. A place to pause, to find her bearings.

Blinding white flashed, and she fell with a cry.

## CHAPTER 16. – ROKURA

Rokura could not move.

Not even the Viareya people of the far north and their Shifting Faces could manage such a thing. How? How had the boy ever lived? Was the poor lad cursed? Had some enormous, undeserved cruelty been inflicted upon him by the Gods?

Rokura exhaled slowly.

He would find no answers kneeling before the pale corpse. Best to return the strange boy, who was clearly not Fara, to the peace of his grave.

He pushed a pile of soil back across the boy's legs. "Forgive me for disturbing your slumber."

*Please.*

Rokura paused. Had a voice... spoken within his mind? So faint that he might have imagined –

*Please help me.*

He turned but there was no-one. Before him, the boy's body remained deathly still, and there was work to be finished. Besides, a voice speaking within his mind, that was not possible.

*More... sunlight.*

"Who speaks?" he demanded, muscles tensing.

*Please!*

The voice echoed fainter, as if dwindling away to nothing, but with the word came the certainty that the *boy* spoke. Somehow, it was the pale youth who called for help!

Impossible…

But Rokura scraped at the dirt anyway, digging with his hands until he had freed the lad, lifting him and striding a few paces away to place the young man upon the grass.

Sunlight fell upon him, but at first it seemed to make no difference.

Rokura leant down, and there it was – a hint of movement; the lad's chest began to rise and fall in a steady rhythm. Some faint colour even returned to his skin.

But it was not enough for him to move… or speak again.

Not until late afternoon, when the young man sat up with a shudder.

Rokura looked up from where he was stacking kindling in a shallow fire-pit. With slow movements, the lad brushed at the traces of soil and glanced around, his faceless head seeming well-aware of his surroundings.

Still, how could it be? *How* had such a boy survived – not only being buried, but… at all?

Yet the pale young man was facing him now.

*Thank you for saving me.*

Rokura smiled, though he could not be sure the lad would know. "I am relieved to see you've recovered. I am Rokura."

*My name is Iggy.*

There were dozens of questions to choose from, like the way the sun had seemed to revive him or the ability to speak without words, but the potential for danger came first. "Do you know who did this to you?"

*No.*

Whoever it was probably assumed the young man was dead. "Are you being hunted, perhaps?"

*Only by exhaustion, I guess.* Even the soundless voice carried a note of bitterness. *Can you tell me where I am?*

"Roughly a week from the eastern coast of Nasaru."

*Is there a river or lake nearby?*

"I have water," Rokura replied, then frowned at his stupidity. How would Iggy even *drink* it? "Unless..."

*It's better if I can submerge myself.*

Iggy stood and took a few wobbly steps that did not inspire confidence.

Taking the boy south while chasing after the rebels was out of the question. Too fragile by far. There *was* a suitable outpost at the Takirov border; the question was whether Iggy would be safe there. Ordering the Nasaru soldiers to protect him might work as a temporary measure, but would the lad remain in danger, considering his appearance?

*I can protect myself.*

Unlikely. "Not in your current state," he replied, trying not to sound too dismissive. And then he blinked. Had the young man read his mind?

*I can. Especially if your thoughts are particularly loud. It's how I can understand you too, since I don't speak Nasaru.*

"I see," Rokura replied with a frown, though it made sense. "Let me take you to an outpost or a town, perhaps. There is one not far from here. They will have water and shelter. In the meantime, I can find something else for you to wear, some better clothing at least. You must be cold."

*Do you have a hood?*

"I probably have an old cloak and hood. It'll do for the meantime but it's not a perfect disguise, if that's what you're seeking."

*Of course.*

"Then will you let me take you somewhere safer?"

*Since I left my home, I have only met those who would do me harm.*

Rokura sighed. "I will not force you to join me but ask, will you let my actions speak for themselves?"

*For now, I will.*

"Then use this," Rokura said as he dropped the last of the kindling and rose, moving to Arrow where he drew a spare cloak from his saddlebag. "Can you ride, Iggy?"

*I don't think so.*

"Then I will carry you," he said. "Simply grip the pommel and I will ensure you do not fall. It will be a bumpy ride at first, but you will grow accustomed."

*Thank you.*

Rokura lifted Iggy into the saddle then climbed up behind him, taking the reins and setting off toward the paved road at a walk.

Iggy did not tense up, nor did he seem too bothered, and so Rokura moved into a trot and then after a time, to a canter.

Instead of conversation, he let the clap of the paved road beneath Arrow's hooves echo in the failing light. The city of Mamoya was still some distance away but if nothing else, the wooden disc from Eroya confirmed the rebels continued south toward the border – no change in course, and they would have to detour Mamoya themselves.

Despite his earlier rush of confidence, stopping the slavers before they reached the mountain pass might no longer be an option – not without support and time to coordinate it – even before discovering Iggy. But King Mutolo had been *very* clear about wanting answers; not just exactly what was going on, but the names of leaders and traitors along with a location for the rebel stronghold.

Mamoya would be a useful point from which to gather information, then set off once more.

But first, locating a decent campsite.

By the time he found one, in a small hollow some distance from the highway, and once the tent had been pitched and Arrow fed, Iggy was moving only slowly beneath the setting sun. Yet the lad still managed to request use of the pot before it was set over the flame. *If I plunge my hand into water, it will allow me to drink, in a way.*

"Oh. Please," Rokura said, handing over the pot, which was not half full.

When young man placed his hand within and sat, his shoulders relaxed a little. Within moments, he handed the pot back and it was near-empty.

*Thank you.*

Rokura refilled the pot from his store. "The wells of Mamoya will have plenty of water. Some inns even have baths that we might well use."

*That would be easier but I am not certain. I know the town will not welcome me.*

He could not disagree, and nor was it becoming to lie. "I would protect you, should you choose to venture within. Perhaps I could bring you water and a better disguise."

*I will sleep upon your offer.* And then the young man sought shelter of the tent.

Rokura kept his sigh very soft as he brewed tea, having no appetite for an actual meal. Iggy's distrust was certainly strong, yet could any blame him? It seemed he had suffered not only in recent times – there was a skittish quality that lurked beneath his weariness. *Just what drove him to the plains in the first place? And from where?* Could the lad have come from one of the islands? From across the sea? He did not seem to be from Senoja, at least, not considering the way he 'spoke' Nasaru.

Which left the Inora, surely?

Perhaps a more pressing question – who had buried him?

But neither Rokura's tea nor the falling darkness offered any answers, and after checking upon Arrow, he soon took his own rest, stretching out upon his bedroll and closing his eyes.

A sweet voice woke him.

It was singing; her clear notes skipping along the scales, nimble and hypnotic.

When Rokura opened his eyes and rose, half a smile upon his lips, the embers in the campfire had changed to a deep pink. Flames wavered, slowly as if under water, casting light that seemed to stick to every surface, soft as pollen, gleaming upon the stones, the cookware and Iggy, even Rokura's own hands when he raised them.

Her song drew nearer.

Rokura rose to one knee, straining his eyes in the dark – if only he could catch a glimpse of the singer!

As he stood, his hand brushed the hilt of a blade and he blinked.

Something was not right.

Why had the firelight changed? *Who* was singing? From where? The scent of lilac and... chocolate lay heavy upon the air but when her voice rose into a crescendo, it was the beauty of the song that had him holding his breath.

She was already standing in the camp.

Her gown was of a bleeding pink, lace clinging to her curves; flared sleeves adorned with gleaming pearls and a blushing gemstone at her throat.

And finally, a grinning skull atop her smooth neck.

It too, gleamed.

*Danger, danger, danger...*

But when she lifted a hand and beckoned Rokura closer, he strode forward without hesitation. Disobedience would only upset her.

"Join me." Her soft hand brushed against his, and with only slight effort, she pulled him near.

Up close, her eye-sockets were filled with black pollen.

"Take your rest, warrior. You have earned it, without reservation."

He leant closer to hear her voice, for it was soft and gentle and each word was a gift, like a truth that others had never seemed to offer. His knees wavered, and she took him into her arms, setting him down on the cool earth and supporting herself next to him with one arm, using the other hand to stroke his cheek.

Panic fluttered from somewhere deep within but her silken touch dispelled every doubt before it could take hold.

"Be proud of the way you lived."

"Even in light of my mistakes?" he asked, finding his own

voice at last.

Her tone was impossibly forgiving. "Who has never once spoken or acted in error?"

Somehow, the truth of her words was undeniable... could it be... even when it came to Oyo and Jabarin, was such a thing true, even then? The old, dull ache of grief returned, coupled with the echo of crashing waves...

The night snapped into cold stillness.

Her dress drained of colour between one blink and the next, and a heaviness filled the air. It squeezed, hard enough to push his limbs together – and then nothing.

# CHAPTER 17. – ROKURA

Rokura lay upon the cool earth, breathing hard. His ears were ringing and his vision was a jagged passage of pink and blinding white, the pain of whatever exactly had happened stabbing at his skull… but not limited to his head either.

What *was* clear was the fact that his young charge could obviously take care of himself, in certain situations. *Not that I'm complaining, since he certainly saved me.*

It had taken some time after Iggy's intervention to realise the lad had broken whatever spell the spectre cast. And just as much time passed before his shuddering eased, when he realised exactly how close he'd come to disaster.

And all of it owed to the mysterious stranger's power.

Still, *something* had led to Iggy becoming so frail and weakened that he was mistaken for a corpse and buried… or perhaps worse, there was something out there stronger than Iggy. But for now, that didn't seem so pertinent. For now, the details about Iggy's own power had to be understood.

Especially since the firelight had returned to its usual colours, and the strange siren-creature was gone. It took a moment for Rokura to realise that a skull of bleached pink rested in his hands.

He flinched and set the skull down beside him. Then he reached for a nearby stone, one with an adequate heft, and lifted it. Best to be certain.

*Do not destroy the skull, Rokura.* Iggy's voice echoed within his mind.

The lad moved around the campfire slowly, coming to kneel beside Rokura.

"Why?" It was the only word he could speak, though as before, his questions were plentiful. What was the creature and where had it come from? Precisely how had Iggy banished her? Again, his powers obviously extended beyond the ability to speak via telepathy... not dissimilar to Senoja. The young man *had* to be from Nokema.

Being thrust into such unnatural realms, the uncertainty of it all, was not a welcome event. So much was impossible to predict, quite unlike war. Or even political manoeuvring, both of which were all too similar.

*I have a feeling, that's all. I can't explain it, but when I lashed out... it seemed like she receded. She was attacking us, but I think we have an understanding now.*

Rokura narrowed his eyes. "That makes no sense, lad."

*Still, I don't think there's any need to act in haste.*

"This skull is clearly dangerous."

*Not to me.*

Rokura exhaled. Perhaps he was correct, and while Rokura did not smash the skull, he did not release the stone either. Taking the lad to Mamoya on the morrow or sending him on his way with the skull would remove the immediate threat, if the pale pink bone *did* still pose a danger, but that only removed a threat to himself.

Others would remain at risk if the siren awakened.

"That cannot be my only concern. Others would be in danger," Rokura said as he raised the hunk of stone.

The rock flew from his grip.

*I said no.*

Iggy rose and Rokura matched his movement, and though he did not reach for any weapon, his frown was deep. The lad could strike without appearing to even move – there was no need to antagonise him any further. But nor did such a thing mean travelling with a creature that could so easily ensnare people. "I will not take you to Mamoya, not with that skull."

*Then leave us behind.*

"I see." How sudden, the end of his role attempting to protect the lad. *Nor will I learn the truth about him, it seems.* Rokura stepped away from the skull. "It is yours."

Iggy collected the skull and started from the camp, heading for the highway with swift steps, his slight form pale in the darkness.

Before he had gone too far, Rokura called after. "Wait. Take some water."

The strange young man turned back. *You do not need to worry about me.*

Rokura found a flask and jogged forward, reaching Iggy quickly and handing over the water. "That might be true but I'm sure I will, nevertheless. If you travel east of here, you should reach one of the streams that feeds into the Bright River sometime tomorrow."

Iggy hesitated, then accepted the flask. *Thank you.*

The young man resumed his walk, shortened cloak stirring

as a wind rose. Rokura watched Iggy until he disappeared from sight, then shook his head as he returned to his bedroll; leaving the tent for packing away in the morning.

There was a chance the mysterious young man might survive, powerful as he was... even with the strange skull in hand, but the king's business would remain first priority.

*****

The city of Mamoya overlooked an empty stretch of land lined by painted gravestones that in turn rested beneath the mountain pass leading south to Takirov. It was a mammoth stone wall that climbed quickly to cover half the sky, the sun only now sneaking above its rim.

Rokura leant against the parapet, staring down at the graves. They did not block the paved highway, instead leaving plenty of room for merchant trains to pass into the city, their wagons mostly laden with Black Coral bound for markets far and wide. And of course, being such an important resource, the merchants were well-protected by guards – often royal soldiers clothed in red cloaks.

It did not seem that those passing the rows of graves took much notice, though of course from such a distance, it was impossible to tell. Each grave represented a Takirov family slaughtered in one war or another, but new wreaths of thorns had been appearing over the years, placed on behalf of those killed in more recent violence.

"I'd burn them all if I could," the sergeant standing nearby said with a sneer upon his broad face, red cloak thrown open to reveal mail and sword belt. The other soldiers glanced at the man.

"Not I," Rokura replied. Each life commemorated was still

a life, even if the rebels of the day and soldiers of the past had committed their own murderous acts. And there had been no shortage of such.

"Don't tell me you're some Taki-lover," the man said, then added an honorific when Rokura turned to stare.

"Sergeant Mileka, was it?"

"Yes, My Lord."

"I will afford you my grace, but only once. I will even answer your churlish question and say that I would rather spend time on something to memorialise our fallen. If that satisfies you, Sergeant, then find me the Prime Scout as requested."

"Of course," the man stammered, then set off at a brisk walk.

While the Scout was probably already well on the way to the walls, Sergeant Mileka had worn out his welcome in record time. *What was the governor thinking, saddling me with such a fool?*

He turned from the border to stare down at the buildings now. Little about the garrison-city spoke of grace or beauty – hard lines everywhere, precise angles from the patterned streets set in rectangles. The buildings, too, whether single storey or greater, whether market or row of homes, whether square plots of brick-work enclosing small gardens of muted greens… all hard lines.

From his vantage point, it seemed little colour filled the town.

Such a thought was an exaggeration, considering the deep blues, maroons and oranges visible above some inns or in flags that lined the streets, yet Mamoya was no Festival-City Omaila either.

Guard posts stood at regular intervals along the same streets, larger in the few squares he could see, but no part of

Mamoya contained so many soldiers as the barracks; men and women in armour and red and white tunics moved about in the yard, glimpses of steel flashing in the tiny gaps between planks upon the scaffolding. Two score soldiers at least filed into the yard, boots creating a cacophony upon the stones as they gathered before a heavyset man bearing the single wing of a sergeant.

But Rokura did not listen; he was counting rooms and windows. The garrison had been expanded since his last visit; now Mamoya hosted at least a thousand troops. Enough that any attacking force from Takirov could not afford to ignore.

Such an assault remained unlikely, for now.

And if the rebels had actually managed to capture Asaro Itonye by chance or design, then they would not need to launch a full assault. King Mutolo would have to bargain. Or strike back. Would Mutolo be just as willing to avenge a corpse, to use the death of his unacknowledged son to launch an attack? The man was measured but could be quick to fury.

Rokura heaved a sigh as he turned back to the open stretch of land before the mountains; clear of any tree, shrub or stone large enough to hide behind. Had the rebels crossed it or sought some hidden path across the border? Reports suggested no traces, but the Prime Scout would hopefully have more information.

When the man, Lettaka, arrived, still dressed in deep brown and grey, it was with an apologetic bow. "I'm sorry, My Lord. But we found nothing that suggested the passage of such a party as you seek." Unlike most other soldiers, his moustache had been bleached somehow, though his short, brown hair was more traditional. Of course, his appearance mattered little if he could perform his task well.

"If they did come this way, are there paths or passages that could grant them access to the south? Without taking an extremely long detour?"

Lettaka pointed west of the highway toward a gorge lined by dark fir trees, where fewer gravestones waited. "That gorge runs along the mountain for some miles, a thin stream at its bottom. It eventually plunges beneath the earth but impressive climbing equipment would be needed to reach any underground passage, if one exists."

Rokura nodded. "Anything else?"

The Prime Scout rubbed at his chin. "Not unless they're planning to sail around the reefs."

"And there were no traces upon the plain?"

"None." There was no hesitation in his voice.

"Perhaps they have turned back, then." Rokura leant against the parapet. "My thanks for your time, Lettaka."

The Prime Scout offered a short bow as he departed, and Rokura finally returned indoors, striding down bare halls toward the meeting room where Governor Conisz would likely be waiting.

Thankfully, the governor had remained in the large room. His narrow face was lit by a many-chambered Coral-lamp where it hung over a table that dominated the room. Boasting only chairs and a single cabinet full of rolled maps, the table's surface free of all but a single ledger.

Upon the page were two words only – Border Crossings – and the number twenty-two for the tenth week of spring. Yet, there was a careful but still noticeable tear in the ledger.

Conisz gestured for Rokura to sit when he arrived. "I fear

your enquires were not fruitful?"

"Not precisely."

"Then I hope I have an answer that will satisfy. I only apologise for not considering it sooner – what of a border crossing in disguise, staggered in small enough numbers to avoid too much scrutiny?"

Rokura stroked his beard. "An interesting possibility."

"A possibility only, I must add."

"Perhaps my quarry has not attempted deception at the border, after all," Rokura said, allowing a touch of regret to enter his voice as he perused the list. And it was not entirely an act, for it had been his best idea to answer the mystery. *Perhaps there is more afoot here.* "No group so large has even attempted a crossing."

The governor was hiding something.

"Sadly no," Conisz agreed. "But on the morrow, please let me lend you Lettaka and his men – if they cannot find any traces of those you seek, then none can beyond the king's own Hounds of Malice."

If nothing else, the disc from Sorcerer Eroya still urged a southern course. "I suspect the Hounds are otherwise occupied, so I will be glad of Lettaka's assistance."

"Of course. I suppose the Hounds are busy with Sulo in the western slums?"

"I am afraid the king has not seen fit to share such things with even me," Rokura replied.

"Certainly, Lord Rokura," Conisz said as he moved to the cabinet and locked the ledger within.

Rokura rose. "You have my thanks."

The governor escorted him to the door and in the hallway,

said his goodbyes before striding off toward a stairwell. Rokura watched the man leave. Before dawn, he would take another look at the ledger. If nothing else, it might confirm some suspicions. A page had been torn free, that much was clear to a trained eye. But exactly *what* was being hidden?

## CHAPTER 18. – THORN

Thorn's first few steps after slipping from a ray of light were always a little uncertain, but it never lasted very long, and he was soon striding along the stone toward a dark entry set in the mountain range, cloak trailing him.

Beyond the range waited the Valley, and if he had wished to travel far enough – Nokema Rikhen itself. Home. Or at least, it was home a *very* long time ago. And where the village stood now was not its first locus, either. *But why visit such a gravesite?*

He passed into shadow, the chill that followed enough for him to sigh.

Or perhaps the sigh was more to do with what had been lost.

Most likely, a lingering, even misplaced bitterness.

After all, had the Guardians actually kept their ancient promises, nothing that was about to happen would have been possible. *In their failure, I succeed.*

They should have been vigilant, should have been ready to fight instead of staring into the reflections they cast upon their ever-shrinking world. Sometimes, it was surprising to learn that Nokema still permitted merchants.

*Maybe they deserve their fates.*

He paused to drink from his flask before striding deeper, drawn toward the depths of the Moon Gate where his target waited. And this time, he would break the last of the Seal. After, only one would remain. A hundred years of planning – and lying – were finally coming to an end.

His step quickened. Before total dark, he pulled a pendant from his shirt, a necessary crutch, in such a place. The pale Glow-Coral revealed rough-hewn walls and little else. No matter. Nor had it ever really mattered, since the call of the Moon Father would soon lead him down familiar passages, down familiar stairwells carved with warnings and then to the half-buried well and small altar.

The warnings continued down and eventually into the vaulted chamber. They had been carved into the flagstones in both Old Senoja and Nokema too, joined by an unseen but barrier that was easily bypassed, like slipping between strands of a web. But he had never bothered to break it, since it did enough to deter the unwary.

"At last."

He approached the well and altar where both lay half-buried in black soil that was always moist, always crawling with undying insects, always full of tiny, rotting flowers of a flat grey.

Perhaps the only mystery in the place.

But probing it was not a requirement. All he need do was stand within, long enough to blacken the final row of opal.

Thorn strode to the altar, boots sinking into the soil, the rich scent almost enough to have him gag. He sunk nearly to his knees. The damp pressed its way through his pants, and the

tiny legs of insects brushed against him but caused no pain –
at least, would not, so long as he worked swiftly.

"Another step closer, Ibila," he murmured.

He lifted both hands and rested them upon the opals that
had been set into the altar. Each was arranged so that together,
they formed a face – the stern gaze of the Sun Goddess. Yet
few of the milky rainbows gleamed in response to his Glow-
Coral, a testament to progress made over decades of visits.

*Once more.*

Power built within him, soon enough it caused sweat to
trickle down from his temples; quite the trial to do so in the
Moon Gate. But he drew more, letting it seep into his arms
and hands, to his fingers where the tips brushed against the
smooth gemstones.

Carefully, carefully, he released some.

An opal grew dark.

Not with a bang or a blast, not with burst of light either –
another piece of the Seal not only broken but stolen.

And now Thorn no longer found himself sweating from
effort as he burnt another opal, stealing its stored magic and
repeating the process again and again until only one remained.
He took but a single extra moment to hold back something
for the aftermath, then blackened the final opal.

The Glow-Coral flickered… and then nothing.

Yet the Seal was broken, the soil had fallen silent and still.

He slumped against the altar. A smile rested upon his face
as he simply breathed, taking his time to recover enough to
rise. Even the earthy scent was fading, vanishing along with
the last of the barriers to his goal.

When he did rise, dirt trailing, he stumbled free of the altar and started back toward the stairs without a backward glance.

In time, the next Seal could be broken. First, it was best to avoid the coming Grains, which would soon begin to seep from the altar. Quite slowly at first, but if left unchecked, in numbers likely to overwhelm the Valley in a matter of nights.

The Moon Father would be focused upon the Kaarsi Seal in Senoja, now.

While recovery after breaking a Seal was not swift, it would allow time to complete the Coral Tree; a step in his plan that could not be skipped.

Without the Tree, the Moon Father could not be harvested – that would mean a failure in every way.

By the time Thorn reached the stairs, he was already preparing to speak to Ibila, though the chances of her hearing him were far better from outside the range, free from the interference of relics that lingered from a time when the Guardians were vigilant.

When he finally did drag himself from the Dalma Mountains that sheltered Nokema and the Inora, he had used the last of what he had stolen from the opal. But now, the sunlight was feeding him once more. He lifted his face and opened his palms, standing still to absorb everything he could.

Strength flowed through his limbs and he straightened, bringing Ibila to mind, her shape and scent, her face, her smile, her dark eyes, so that it would not be impossible to imagine she in fact stood at his side despite there being but a patch of greying grass and little else.

"Ibila." He did not bother to send his voice with his gift; the Twining had not faded.

*Mutolo, you succeeded?*

"I did. Tell me, has Lord Onga taken the bait?"

*Eagerly.*

"And who did he run to this time?"

*General Tahbe. To convince him that funds will be taken from the military to complete the Tree.*

"Ah. He is getting desperate, then."

*Because you still have Tahbe's support.*

"I do." Tahbe expected the Coral Tree could be used as a weapon, if needed, and for once it had not been necessary to lie. Not insomuch as the potential use of the Coral Tree truly *could* be a weapon. Potential only, since it wouldn't survive what he had in mind.

*There is also a message from Lok. She has finally found them.*

Thorn clenched his hand; a third triumph! "Where?"

*One is actually in Valley and the other Nasaru. They appear to be siblings, just as you predicted.*

Now he began to stride along the road. Waiting generations for the right pair to be born in the village certainly offered a satisfying rush of triumph. *Especially with such perfect timing.* "I will return and find a way to bring them together, but first I need to make a short detour."

*For how long?*

"It is lovely that you miss me."

*And I know you have been thinking of me, so try not to sound too smug.*

"A fine answer," he replied with a chuckle. "I would say a day at the most."

*Wonderful, Your Majesty. Bring me back something sweet, won't you?*

## CHAPTER 19. – MEI

A throbbing pain in her temples woke Mei with a groan. She turned, even flipping her pillow for the cooler side, but sleep was now out of reach. *Looks like I have no choice.* She pushed aside her blankets and fumbled for the water she kept on the bedside table, eyes still half-closed to the dim room.

Her hands found air only.

Mei sat upright, fast enough to wince in pain.

She was in a bed covered with furs, warm colours of timber walls surrounding her. It took a moment, but when she finally noticed the walls curved up from the ground to become the roof, she blinked. *What a strange room.* Light snuck in via a pair of small windows, looking more like teardrops. Had they not been shuttered, they probably would have offered a lot more illumination.

A single table stood bolted to the floor opposite, a closed door beyond.

"Hello?"

No answer. Mei stood, and the room spun. She slumped back until the dizziness faded. *What happened?* She raised a hand to the bandage on her head... Bandage? Wait... last night, her flight through the forest! *I ran into a tree… didn't I?*

Adrenaline surged and the throb of pain grew more pronounced. But she took a moment to breathe deeply, to wait for her mind to still enough that the pain eased.

But concern had not faded. Who had owned that light? Had the same person brought her to the room to rest? Or for some dark purpose? *If they did, they didn't bother binding me.* Mei took a few steps into the room, finding her possessions at the foot of the bed.

She knelt by her pack and rifled through it. Nothing amiss. Her father's blade, Iggy's carving and the pouches Arun had given her were in their place too, tied to her belt where it in turn lay beside her cloak. Even that had been folded neatly.

Mei took the dagger after a moment's hesitation and walked into a dark hallway.

The blade was better than nothing; the pain in her head suggested that using her telekinesis would come at a heavy price.

In one direction, the hall led to two other rooms – one full of barrels, none of which she opened, and the other room a far larger space. It contained a simple kitchen and a worn armchair of deep brown fur arranged beneath two circular windows.

Morning light poured in but revealed no real clues as to the owner's identity. Mei crept back along the passage, passing the room where she'd woken, and stopping at a frame of white light that seemed to burn through gaps in construction. Another door.

She pushed it open and found an entryway with a second door and window.

There, a dun-coloured cloak with a wide hood hung on

a peg, while another held a quiver of arrows bearing white feathers. Mei paused to listen but heard nothing. She was alone, it seemed. She paused to examine the stitching on the cloak as it was not the typical two-coloured, cross-pattern used in the village.

"Who lives here?" Mei lifted the latch and pushed her way out into daylight.

Outside, the sun penetrated the canopy and she squinted against it, welcome though the rays were to her skin.

Blossoms from the Pilor tree gleamed. The chatter of birds, joined by rasping from a grey branch-glider, drifted across a broad clearing of grass. A low wall of uneven stones sheltered a vegetable garden nearby, but the open space she stood within was dominated by the strange dwelling she'd just left.

It had the vague look of a huge onion with windows and a chimney, save for the twine running from one point, where clothing had been hung to dry... hard to tell from each item who the owner might be. The building was nothing like the circular mud-brick homes the Inora built, and nothing like what Denuko described of Nasaru structures either. She approached a nearby water barrel. The surface was still, the cup sitting atop it bone dry. No-one had used it recently; she was alone.

"So, you're awake. How do you feel?"

Mei spun.

A tall woman approached from between the trees, an amused expression on her otherwise stern face. Dressed in leather breeches and a tunic that must have once been blue but was now closer to grey, she carried a short bow and a brace of rabbits slung over a shoulder. With her green eyes and flaxen braid, she could have been from Nokema.

Drawing near, a sense of forcefulness was clear but the woman studied Mei without any sense of menace. "Did you sleep well?"

"I did. And thank you for helping me," Mei said. *Do I not need the knife, after all?* "I'm Mei of the Inora."

The woman chuckled. "That I can see. And you are welcome. Lucky I found you when I was checking my snares. You're not much of a traveller, are you? Come inside. I bet you're hungry."

Mei glanced away. *I'll seem even stupider if she knows I ran into a tree.* "I am hungry. Thank you for your hospitality."

"Wait until you taste my cooking. It may not live up to your expectations," the woman replied and this time Mei caught a hint of an accent but she could not place it. No surprise; she'd heard so few in the Valley.

"Do you live here alone... ah, *Han-ja?*" Mei asked, using a formal address, unsure of what to call this woman.

"Han-ja?" She paused at the door, her face thoughtful. "Older woman, right?"

"It's a sign of respect," Mei added quickly.

She opened the door and led Mei inside. "I remember now. One of your Exiles taught me your language long ago, girl. Call me Jeniva. I imagine it's easier on us both."

After a moment's hesitation, Mei started down the dim passage to the kitchen, where she stood by the door. Should she sit? Jeniva had waved her on and was now depositing her bow in the hall, adding a second quiver to the first.

After a moment, the woman grunted in satisfaction before carrying the rabbits into the kitchen, where she set to skinning them with a long blade produced from her belt. Spots of blood occasionally dripped to the floor as she worked, dropping the skins into a bucket and placing the flesh onto a chipped plate.

"You can sit, Mei of the Inora," Jeniva said over her shoulder.

Mei did so, finding the old chair quite comfortable. "Thank you." She blinked when the woman swore, stamping a booted foot, but whatever bothered her did not seem to vex her long. "Where am I, if I might ask?"

"The Glass Forest, of course."

"Am I near the Moon Gate?"

"Two hours east of here. Just follow the river."

Mei straightened. "That's wonderful. Can you tell me, have you seen anyone else from the village lately? I'm looking for my brother."

"Sorry, girl. I haven't seen anyone for months, and that was a merchant at that. Your brother heading for the Gate?"

"He was, yes."

"I don't remember any of the Inora going through the Gate for a long time," Jeniva said. "Not that I see all who pass through."

"That's where Iggy's going. He made a boat and I believe he took it to the Gate."

Jeniva turned. "A boat?"

Mei nodded.

"Once we eat, I must show you something."

"What is it?"

"After we eat," Jeniva said. Mei opened her mouth but the woman's eyes offered no room for argument. "You need some food, girl."

Mei settled back into the chair, curbing her impatience – and worry.

Despite Jeniva's warning, the woman's cooking was delicious. Not the rabbit so much as the added rosemary and lemongrass, and it should not have been a surprise. After all, Jeniva, who obviously lived alone, relied on herself for everything. She would have hunted and cooked, repaired her home, maintained her weapons, tended her garden. Her face was a little weathered and she had calloused hands with dotted tattoos on their backs, and her mannerisms brought Galarik to mind. "It's close to something called 'vona', a meal from my homeland," Jeniva explained as she washed the dishes.

"Have you been gone for many years?"

"Yes."

"Oh." Mei glanced away at the trace of pain in Jeniva's voice. "Did you, ah, build this place yourself?"

Now Jeniva smiled. "Can you not recognise it?"

"Not really."

Jeniva leant back in her chair. "Let me tell you a tale that explains this place, then. Long ago in Senoja, the land of your ancestors, there was a great thief. Mesike, or 'Liar' is what they called him after his death."

Mei leant forward. "I remember Mesike. He stole the crown of the first Nasaru king, a priceless heirloom. Denuko told me once."

"That he did. Mesike stole some of the most precious things the world has ever produced: the Cresideth Star, a religious artefact that could heal the sick with its light; the Mask of Aehtu, the sleeping face of a God, which was said to grant great wisdom to whoever wore it. These and many other things both valuable and rare." Jeniva paused to drink, as though not used to speaking aloud so much.

"He lived for the thrill of thievery. He loved the chase, the challenge of discovering and removing that which was hidden. And the more foolhardy the better, for the great thief. His undoing came at the height of his conquests, when he had supposedly grown bored, when he thought he'd stolen everything worth taking. One day he agreed to steal Senoja's youngest daughter, the Princess Shar, on the bequest of a jealous sorcerer. Using all his skill, Mesike accomplished the feat and fled with the princess to his keep in the mountains."

Mei frowned. This was new, compared to what she'd heard from Denuko. "And she let him?"

"Supposedly. It was not an easy trip, no. But he then crossed the desert by magical means, and delivered Shar to the sorcerer, only to be betrayed by the powerful magic-user who handed the thief over to the Senoja. Mesike was hung by the Emperor and no-one ever found his treasures. Today, Mesike means 'Liar' because the great thief had once sworn never to steal from Senoja."

Mei was silent a moment. Was such a fantastical tale true? And, more importantly, how did it explain Jeniva's home? Mei gestured to the walls. "I don't know how the story is connected."

"My home is part of *The Swan*, which was the magical ship he used to fly across the desert – the ship he stole from Captain Makkoch of the Takirov."

Mei straightened. "The ship could fly?"

"So the legend goes," Jeniva replied with a shrug. "However it happened, this is the ship, exactly where it crash-landed many years later."

Mei turned in her chair to scrutinise the wooden walls... aside from the shape, they seemed so ordinary. "How?"

"I have Makkoch's log, among those of later captains. They name the ship *The Swan* and detail many voyages, both through air and sea," she said, then finished her drink. "It took me years to decipher the old language, to be honest, and there are many entries I cannot read, even today. But we sit in the crew's cabins even now. I knocked out several of the walls myself when I first found the ship, a half-buried ruin stuck in two centuries worth of dirt and leaves."

"How long ago was that?" Mei asked, awe in her voice.

"That I came here?" Jeniva asked. "Many years ago. You would have been but a babe." She stood and nodded to Mei's own cup. "Have you finished?"

"Yes, thank you."

"Very well. Gather your things, Mei, for I think it's time you continued your journey to the Gate."

*Iggy!* "You said you wanted to show me something about my brother?"

"I do. Come with me when you're ready."

Mei went to Jeniva's bedroom and gathered her possessions, examining her father's blade a moment. Leaving it behind, leaving it for Jeniva, was that an option? *She* would have no trouble using the weapon... But even as Mei pushed down unpleasant thoughts of Aunt Wifral, she strapped the blade to her belt.

Whether Siratta's story about how her ancestors came to possess the weapon was true or not, did not matter. *I can't give away a link to Father.*

"Ready?" Jeniva called.

Mei finished up, striding through the ancient ship to follow the tall woman outside. Jeniva was already at the tree line, bow and quiver added to her own pack.

"What did you find?" Mei asked as she passed the vegetable garden and entered the cooler woods where the sun did not penetrate so far.

"Something you should see. Perhaps an ill omen, perhaps not."

Mei clenched her hand as she followed, a nagging worry growing.

Jeniva moved through the trees swiftly, using a trail she'd obviously worn-in over the years. The murmuring of the river grew as they strode deeper. Mei had no idea where she was in relation to the road, but Jeniva was hardly going to become lost.

It did not take long to reach the Inrik. This deep within the Glass Forest, the river was a wide, powerful creature. It charged through pillars of wood, foaming white where rapids formed as the water disappeared into gloom from a dense stretch of Pilor and pine trees.

The archer stopped.

"Is this it?" Mei asked.

"Up ahead." She pointed. "See, near the bank."

Mei dashed forward, stumbling to a halt at the water's edge.

Splinters lay spread across the grassy bank, joined by chunks of wood too, and in the water, caught between jagged stone, was a shattered prow peeking from the white. It bobbed and shifted, as if trying to keep its head above the water. "Ig."

## CHAPTER 20. – MEI

Droplets of water fell from Mei's hand as she hefted a hunk of wood from the river's shallows, unable to speak. Was it Iggy's boat? Or one owned by some other unfortunate soul? The pieces on the bank had not been exposed to the elements long enough to fade in colour... she stared into the current.

"No, forgive me – come, it is here, something else," Jeniva said from where she gestured to the tree line.

"What?"

"Tracks."

Mei strode after, a dark weight lifting with each step.

Jeniva knelt to point to the ground. "They head toward the Gate, it would seem. If so, he may be in danger now, in the lands Beyond." Heel-prints were still visible where they'd sunk into the soft earth on the riverbank. By the size they could have been made by Iggy.

Mei couldn't hold back a smile, though it was still tempered by concern. "What caused his boat to break?"

"Hard to say. But if it was your brother, I believe he travelled this way two days ago. You will see more evidence soon, trampled flowers and strips torn from the bark. And at one point, a fallen tree."

A familiar outburst? "Iggy sometimes has trouble controlling his power."

"More evidence mounts," Jeniva said as she started along the animal trail. "And few travel the forest I have to say, even Exiles rarely visit over the last few years."

"Someone else seemed to be travelling last night. I don't think it was Iggy at all. I saw their light, off in the trees."

Jeniva paused. "What?"

"Whoever it was carried a light low to the ground, but I never could catch up to them. That's where I was headed when you found me."

She gripped Mei's arm. "You saw what?"

"A steady light, close to the ground," Mei replied, concern growing at Jeniva's gaze. "No matter how fast I walked I couldn't catch it. I, ah, eventually ran into a tree."

Jeniva reached back and drew an arrow, casting her eyes across the quiet wood as she set the shaft to her bowstring. "You may be luckier than I thought."

"Why?"

"That light is something I have only seen once before. And it was not pleasant. Come. To be safe, we're going to reach the Gate well before nightfall, and that means pushing ourselves."

"Wait, is Iggy in danger from the light?"

"Judging by his power, probably not."

"Then are we in danger?" Mei said as she hurried after the woman, struggling to keep up. Jeniva walked faster now, movements seeming charged with some additional purpose.

"I don't know. But I wish you had told me about this sooner."

"After I woke, I just assumed it was you. I was relieved to

be safe."

She shook her head. "Well, no matter now."

"What is the light?"

"Something I cannot explain," Jeniva said as she detoured a fallen tree that spanned a gaping hole in the loam. Dirt and grass, leaves and glassy blossoms were strewn about – not unusual for one of Iggy's outbursts. "It was not quite one year after I came here. I was returning from a long hunt and it was still not dawn. At first, I thought the light was a traveller and I sought it out, thinking to assess any threat."

Mei nodded as she listened.

"I could not reach the light at first, and so I followed it further from the trail, never able to gain any ground. In time, I gave up and started back toward the cabin."

"So, you never saw it up close."

"Closer than I'd have liked," she said. "It began to follow *me* after I'd been back on the main road only a short time. As if I'd thwarted it by turning away."

Mei shivered. "Then you saw it?"

"Perhaps not its true form. Up close, it seemed tinted with pale blue and I *thought* I saw serpent-like shapes moving inside the light." Jeniva shook her head. "To this day, I am not certain. A sense of despair flowed forth, sapping the strength from my legs, but I ran. When I saw my ship, I felt no relief. The fear drove me deep inside, and I barricaded the door with barrels." Her eyes continued to rove, going to the river, to Ig's trail and the trees around them. "Having said that, I doubt it will appear in daylight, so we have that in our favour at least."

Mei exhaled softly, her own stride faltering a little. If a woman like Jeniva was worried... And would even someone like Jeniva survive an encounter in the night, on her way home?

The path Ig had taken was not so random for all its violence – it did not stray far from the river, or so Jeniva explained. Mei now had to take the woman's word for any bent stalks or other evidence, as it did not seem enough to suggest his passage, but Jeniva lived in the Glass Forest; she was a hunter, she knew her business.

And Iggy would stick to the Inrik since he had little choice.

The rush and roar of the river grew louder as they neared the Moon Gate, where the current would plunge underground, eventually spewing out onto the Nasaru plains. Pale trees thinned as the earth became rockier, closer to the Dalma Mountains now. Vines grew thick around the base of many rock formations, coiling round nearby trees too – some bearing faint yellow patterns.

"Watch for snakes here," Jeniva said. "They can blend within the vines."

Mei nodded but did not answer. The rising terrain and Jeniva's brisk pace was taking it out of her; she stumbled along with straining lungs. *Clearly, what I think of as steady travel is more like a saunter compared to what Jeniva is used to.*

"Jeniva, I have to rest," Mei said when they topped a small rise. She leant against a boulder and took out her flask, draining it with large gulps. Rays from the sun did not exactly blast down upon her but the sunlight had not disappeared and what remained warmed her limbs, restoring some strength.

Being still always sped up the process a little.

Jeniva glanced over her shoulder. "The Moon Gate is just ahead if you are willing to continue."

Mei pushed herself up with groan, walking on. It was like

wading through heavy mud but she did not stop, keeping her gaze fixed ahead. The Dalma Mountains had been rising between the trees for some time and as they crested a second rise, suddenly the Moon Gate appeared.

An enormous black cavern waited at the foot of the Dalma.

On one side of the cavern, the River Inrik leapt from its banks to plummet into darkness, roaring all the way down into a maze of black echoes. Hugging the opposite wall was the old road, the one Denuko Gree and few other merchants used, boring through the mountain. A broad ledge wide enough for two carts curved away from the gorge where it travelled into the shadows, leading to the world beyond.

And now that Mei stood before it, she clenched her hand in a small gesture of triumph.

Finally.

## CHAPTER 21. – MEI

"Well done, girl," Jeniva said, then pointed to the cavern. "See the carvings? The Moon Gate."

She nodded as they approached. "I remember."

A perfect arch of faded symbols and words spanned the entryway. From bank to bank, the carvings depicted stages of the moon, with the full moon at the peak. Between the circles were runes that bore no resemblance to anything used in Nokema, nor what little she'd seen of the swirling Nasaru writing.

Mei craned her neck and stepped closer, foot striking something hard.

A steel ring had been set into the stony road. She knelt to brush away the dust and gravel, uncovering a second ring around the first. "What is this?" she asked, lifting her voice enough to compete with the waterfall.

Jeniva leant against her bow. "I have noticed it too, but your guess is as good as mine. You've been here before, right?"

"I don't remember too much." Just Siratta and Father speaking in soft voices in the dark, warning her not to tread upon the paths that left the road. Mei held her hands over the inner circle a moment longer. The steel seemed a little too cold? Odd, but probably not important. She stood, glancing back into the cavern. "Do you know if Iggy went through?"

"His trail leads here and I doubt he would have stopped."

Mei looked up at her guide. "Thank you for helping me, Jeniva. I don't know if I would have reached the Gate without you."

"I am glad," she said with a smile. "Now, best you prepare your lantern here."

"Right." Mei slung her pack to the earth and removed the lantern she'd taken from home, checking on the wick first. "What can I expect in there?"

"It is a wide path with many side passages, but I don't advise leaving the road – there's something down in the bowels of this mountain. Halfway in, you will feel it... like a great force on your head, neck and shoulders." She shrugged. "But it passes quickly, and then the earth slopes down toward the plain. It should take the rest of the day to exit the mountain. Then you will be in Nasaru. Seek a traveller's camp just east of the exit."

Mei paused at her work. Denuko had not mentioned the strange pressure. "How many times have you been through?"

"Three times too many," Jeniva said, pressing her lips together.

"You don't like it out there, do you?"

The tall woman raised her faded hood and placed a hand on Mei's shoulder, giving it a squeeze before setting off. "Farewell, Mei of the Inora. I hope you find your brother. You will be in my thoughts."

"Thank you again..." Mei called, then trailed off.

An unblinking light appeared between the trees.

This time, it bore the vague shape of a man.

The bright figure wove a sure way toward them, skimming over the river before coming to a halt on the road where it settled between her and Jeniva. Up close, a luminous dust seemed to trail the shape. It was beautiful… but *inside* the thing something less pleasant seemed to writhe – the glittering scales of serpents.

The gentle swirl of the light was so lovely.

Mei drifted toward the figure. Was it really a threat? It hadn't attacked; it had barely moved at all. In fact, if she could just get close enough to touch it…

Jeniva was waving her arms. "Mei, no!"

The luminous shape expanded as Mei drew near, stretching up to take on the form of a single, large serpent. Shadows flashed across the trunks, shaped like spindly legs and long fingers. A feeling of despair spread itself over the Moon Gate, seeming to suck up the air as it did, but Mei did not falter.

"You must flee," Jeniva shouted, her voice strained.

"I think I see jewels in there… between the fangs. They're so beautiful," Mei said softly, drawing closer still. The sense of despair lingered, as strong as ever, but it no longer seemed important at all.

The serpent opened its mouth wide enough to reveal twin sapphires, carved to resemble pears. Up close, other smaller snakes slithered in circles within the light, scales making a sweet sound. Their hissing too was sonorous, and more – soothing words were buried within.

"They're talking to me. Speaking Inora," Mei said as she reached out for the fruit.

"Mei, I can't hear anything. It's dangerous!"

"We don't have to worry. They've seen Iggy. They can take

me to him..." Mei trailed off as the serpent's song swirled and now the figure grew blazing arms, spreading them in a welcoming gesture.

Tears ran down her cheeks, a shiver of joy tingling across her skin. They could help!

Yet, she could not move.

*Why?*

Mei fought against whatever held her back, wrenching a shoulder free.

But the force did not give up. It dragged her further and further into darkness, away from the luminous being. She cried out as the enchanting light dwindled, winking out in a bitter farewell, helpless against the smothering black.

***

Mei did not know how much time had passed when she regained full awareness, but she found herself shuffling through a darkened cavern, keeping close to Jeniva and the warmth of her steady lamp.

The flame cast moving lights across the surface of the Inrik – or Curajithcan now, no doubt – where the river roared nearby. She could not glance at the surface very long; it was a little too similar to the strange creature that had nearly ensnared her.

Jeniva had saved her life.

Twice.

There was no question of that. And now, in the cool hush of the Moon Gate, everything that had been familiar and comforting about the strange serpent of shimmering sand took on a nightmarish quality.

Thankfully, it had not followed... or if it had, the thing was far behind.

"We'll rest here," Jeniva said, stepping just a few paces into one of the side tunnels, and setting down the lamp. She leant against a wall to lift her water flask. Mei took the wall opposite, the chill of its dark stone making the surface seem even harder. Yet it was part of a long wake-up call.

Jeniva removed bread and cheese from her pack and offered some to Mei. "Do you remember what you said before I pulled you back?"

"I do," Mei replied. "That they were speaking to me. In Inora."

"I have been wondering about that. About why the light seemed to drive me away, and yet you were drawn to it."

Mei paused, cheese halfway to her mouth. "It *sought* me because I'm Inora?"

"Yes. I suspect that might be so." Jeniva's frown suggested she was troubled. "I wonder if it consumes Inora... or people with your gifts. That might explain why I now see so few Exiles, where once I did encounter them more often."

Could such a thing be true? Most Exiles had been sent away before her birth – except for Dieg. And Pedija, who had taken to eating the pets of the village. A shiver ran up Mei's spine and she did not continue at once. "I... I don't know what to believe now. If the spirits of the Inora were trapped inside, they came up with a very specific lie to tell me. Are they so clever? They didn't seem to attract me that first time."

"Maybe that thing's true power is to offer whatever its victim most wants?" Jeniva leant forward. "Something valuable at first, to catch your attention... and then the specific lie when you draw close, like the one about your brother. I think to join them would be to cross to the lands of spirit."

Mei nodded slowly. It made sense, as much any other

explanation. Would Iggy have encountered the thing? *If he did, I get the feeling it wouldn't have tempted him.* "Are we safe here?"

"Sleep if you wish, I will be watching."

"Thank you." Mei took a few more bites of her meal and some water before spreading her bedroll across the chilly floor, then stretched out to close her eyes.

Yet a deep sleep played coy for most of her rest, and when she woke it was with stiff limbs. She rose, blinking against a faint glow from the main passage. Jeniva's shadow moved before the lamp as she paced. "How long did I sleep?" Mei asked.

"Half the night perhaps."

"No sign of the shining serpent?"

"None, but we should leave, if you are able."

"I am." Mei performed a short series of stretches, trying to ease an ache in her neck without much success. Was it the long exposure to darkness? Her limbs did feel a little sluggish. "I'll refill my water."

"Be wary."

Mei nodded as she moved down the passage to kneel by the river. It still churned, but she kept a firm grip on her flask as she leant down to fill it. Despite Jeniva's sensible warning, Mei found herself staring into the darkness, thoughts drifting.

Whether it was the shadowy cavern or even the Moon Gate itself, they were safe for the moment.

But what lay beyond the Gate was the bigger threat, surely?

The world Beyond remained an unknown. Finding Iggy was about to become more difficult; he had so many places he could be headed... so long as he was able to keep reasonably close to the river, at least.

Water splashed at her wrist and she lifted her flask.

That was her one hope – that he would stay near the river. "Iggy, stay safe out there."

## CHAPTER 22. – MEI

Mei stood within the shade of the Moon Gate's exit and stared at the vast Beyond.

A green and grey marsh awaited. Split by a road that was broad but perhaps only adequately maintained, damp clung to everything – the low grass, the stones in the road, the trunks of stunted trees.

The bluish tint to the woods from the Valley was gone here. Instead, a more familiar green held sway, hovering over the murky depths of surrounding pools and narrow channels, diluted by a low-lying grey mist.

The journey through the mountain passage had not been as swift as she'd hoped but it was restful compared to yesterday's flight. Jeniva kept to her own advice, ignoring all side tunnels and rushing them through the strange part of the passage where the air seemed to push down on their heads and shoulders.

And while Jeniva had ground her teeth, Mei had to force herself onward, the weight almost suffocating. Impossible to explain, and nothing anyone in the village had ever mentioned. Nor did her memory of the Rite go so deep into the gate...

Few even spoke about the Beyond at all, let alone specifics about the passage. Even Denuko Gree, who was usually full of stories, had not thought to mention the unusual force. Had Iggy been troubled by it?

"So, what do you think?" Jeniva asked from where she stood nearby. "I'll admit, this isn't the most memorable view for a first glimpse."

"It's not beautiful but... it seems boundless."

The breadth of the land she was about to enter stretched on and on above the mist. Even from her position in the marsh beneath Dalma, she could sense stretching plains beyond the water. Her very mind seemed to shrink back from it. Even her muscles tensed. Somehow Ig would have made his way through the swamp, she was sure, though clean water might have been harder to come by now that the Curajithcan had plunged underground for who knew how long.

But he was smart enough to figure something out. At least, for the water. But what would he do with people? People who would not understand him. People he might hurt.

Or people who would want to hurt *him*.

Mei turned back to the Moon Gate, another truth returning to give her pause.

Wouldn't the lands Beyond have to be her home too? Not just so she could protect Iggy but... Aunt Wifral. It was not possible to return, not now. Mei shuddered as something colder than the breeze tugged at her cloak – fear. Or a sense of loss. Grief, perhaps.

Or maybe desperation.

Travelling the Valley, moving within the confines of the Dalma Mountains, chasing Iggy... at least while she had been doing so, some doubts had been easier to push aside. Now an uncertain future as an outcast and a criminal waited. A stranger only, each and every time she set foot in a new place.

"Malkaha Marsh." Jeniva's voice brought Mei back to the Moon Gate.

"How far does it spread?"

"Some days east and west. About the same north, where the road will lead you onto the Nasaru plains and eventually the Omaila Forest."

Mei slung her pack to the ground and took stock of her water. "And you've been through it? Is any of the water safe to drink?"

"It's easy enough to pass. The road is reliable, if not oft-travelled, and there are streams here and there. Just don't drink from still water unless you absolutely must."

"Right." Mei wrinkled her nose as a breeze whipped up, bringing with it the scent of damp earth and rot. Not like the Valley at all.

"I'm sure you'll return one day, if that's what you're thinking."

Mei looked to the older woman, who seemed able to read her mind. Or maybe just her expression. "Not without Iggy, I hope."

"You'll find him."

"Thank you."

Mei hesitated but before she could speak, Jeniva rested a hand on her shoulder. "I know what you're going to ask but I cannot." She waved an arm in a gesture that seemed to encompass the entire world, rather than only the mist-shrouded swamp. "There's nothing out there for me; I'm happier alone." Now she grinned for the first time. "Besides, you're Inora. You can do things with the power of your mind that few others can even comprehend."

"It doesn't quite feel that way. After all, you had to save me back there."

"No, Mei. *You* need to be strong," she said, giving her a slap on the back. "I can't do that for you – no-one can."

Mei nodded.

"Once you're on the plain, you'll need to hunt and forage for food. Be wary of all you meet. Remember, the Nasaru will take you for Senoja."

"Right."

"Then Travel Beneath the Sun, Mei," Jeniva said. "And bring back your brother; I'd like to meet him."

Mei hesitated, then lifted her belongings and hopped close to catch Jeniva in a hug before the woman could protest. "I will." Then she set off at a jog, her shoes clacking on the rocky road, pack thumping against the small of her back.

She couldn't turn to look over her shoulder, and the faster she walked the easier leaving seemed to be. In such a short time, the gruff woman had come to be a real source of strength and comfort. But Jeniva was right. *I'm not her responsibility and she has her own life. I have to find Ig myself.*

Mei gazed ahead.

The green of the Malkaha Marsh grew close to the road in odd places, clumps of moss and damp undergrowth mixed with gnarled tree stumps, the pools and rivulets a murky green. Or brown.

Stands of trees and low hills were scattered across the marsh too – one bare set of branches had taken a shape not unlike a stooped man leaning on a staff... and as she drew near

Mei blinked.

It had been carved!

She charged forward, skidding to halt in the mud before the trunk. Her hand trembled as she reached out to touch grooves that had undoubtedly been made by human hands.

Iggy?

He *had* made it surely, but why? Was it a message? And if so, to whom? Mei ran her palm over the carving. How long had it taken? The detail was not like his other work but it was clear. She straightened. Whatever the reason, it was a good sign – Iggy had travelled the Marsh.

Mei strode on until noon, barely pausing to eat and drink from what remained of her supplies, but when evening drew close its long shadows and the chill of the marsh rose, weariness took over. She found enough dry fuel for a small campfire and lit it on the only broad patch of firm ground beside the road. Her camp was partially shielded by a low rise but better cover nearby didn't even offer enough room to lie down.

Before eating a cold meal and warm tea, she'd bent close to the water but found only a sludge-filled pool. Hints of movement beneath the surface were not encouraging either, so she drank sparingly from one of her flasks instead. Had Iggy found a clearer stream by moving off the main road? He was usually able to sense water, and there were few other paths but Mei hadn't dared try any.

Malkaha Marsh was a quiet place. The trees, short and sparse, contained no birds. On occasion, thin, splotched otters with their pale-yellow fur or swift lizard-creatures slipped in and out of the water, usually causing but faint ripples.

Just as in the Moon Gate, her sleep was fitful when she

sought rest. She woke several times, not simply to relieve herself but after dreams that offered lingering feelings of dread, even if they lacked detail. *I'm surprised they're not full of luminous snakes. Or Aunt Wifral.*

Once, the moon was reflected in the water where it peeked from a cloudbank and she stared at the silvery surface. It seemed a leering face lay within the shadowy shapes but when she looked up, the same vague pattern was not repeated in the moon itself.

She shrugged as she returned to her bedroll. *Still sleepy, I suppose.*

It was best to forget about such things – rest was more important. Tomorrow, she had to start making up some ground on Iggy.

## CHAPTER 23. – MEI

A chill rose from the earth as Mei crested a short rise the next day. The noon sun barely broke through the grey sky, its colour not so different from the withered trees below.

Creeping mist did not help. It seemed her entire body was growing heavier, craving the rays of the sun as she walked. And while her strength wasn't actually failing – it would take a lot more than clouds to do so – there was no spring to her step. And worse, the faintly noxious scent of the mist had its own unwelcome effect, casting a slight haze across her mind and her senses too. Her footfalls sounded muted, dull, and her thoughts weren't much better... blanketed by the entire swampland.

Mei stopped.

Her thoughts! She slammed a fist into her thigh. "I've been a fool, this whole time!"

*Iggy!*

She screamed his name in her mind, sending it out into air like an arrow.

Without an answer, she called again and then once more, putting all her might into the call, dropping to one knee, but still no response. She stopped to massage her temples when her vision darkened, managing to keep a grip on consciousness.

Long minutes passed before the pain eased and her shoulders slumped.

Back in the Valley, they often communicated over long distances. What did his silence mean? *Aren't I strong enough? Or was he simply too far distant?*

Or hurt… or worse.

"Maybe he's just not answering." Mei forced herself back upright with a sigh, then pulled her cloak tight across her chest.

She forged deeper into the marsh, finding no signs of Iggy's passage now – no destruction or new carvings. The best discovery wasn't until evening; a fast rivulet that offered clearer water, and so she filled an empty flask and began searching for shelter, and for food, perhaps even something to cook, now that she had access to plenty of water.

But by the time night fell across the marsh, like a giant spider lowering its bulk over a hole, she had found nothing. At least, nothing she could eat. There had been an otter, but she couldn't bring herself to stun and kill it, which meant she would soon be going hungry. *I have at least one meal left.*

Without stars above, the only light came from her fire, and Mei could well imagine the myths of her people. The Paragons taught that not all Guardians who watched over the Inora were dispassionate observers who judged but rarely intervened. At night, the Guardian Kinnea stretched over the world to observe with her dozens of starry eyes, and day only came when Taiyo, the Sun, chased her away with his fiery arms. Sometimes his work was without flaw and the sky was clear blue, and sometimes the tatters of her web could be seen as drifting clouds.

Easy to believe such myths now, alone in a dark swamp.

A voice drifted through the mist.

Mei froze. The voice was that of a man, speaking a language she did not understand. Other voices answered, and by their tone, they seemed to be arguing. More, their words carried the flowing sound of the Nasaru tongue. First Jeniva's warning and then Denuko's words rang in her mind. *Any soldier worth his salt will pick you up as a spy the moment he lays eyes on you.*

Were they soldiers or merely travellers?

And had they already seen her fire?

She scrambled for water but the men were already so close – even as she fell back, four indistinct figures appeared in the fog, each shape carrying a light. No time to gather belongings! Mei ran, cold air tearing at her throat with each shadowy obstruction she leapt over, with each twist she made to avoid a tree, stone or pool's edge, all the while guided by her mind as much as her vision.

But she couldn't run forever. In time, she'd wear herself out and risk serious injury.

Especially at night.

*Find somewhere to hide, fool!*

Something large loomed ahead – stone, mud and ferns rising up in a huge mound. She slid behind it, pressing herself against the cold moss and holding her breath. Her boots sunk into the earth but found solid ground before the muck reached her calves.

A shout came from the direction of her camp.

Mei peered around the stone.

It was hard to tell, but the light seemed to suggest at least two men striding along the road, nearing but not quite moving in her direction. With at least four voices co-ordinating the search, where were the others? In her camp? Only two held lanterns now but how many would be carrying weapons at their belts? Swords or knives?

In the poor light, few impressions were clear – until the figures drew closer. Swords hung at their sides, broad shoulders and thick arms suggesting men of war, perhaps. She closed her eyes and muttered a prayer to the Guardians.

The voices were closing in.

Mei peered around the ferns and muffled a gasp – one man was almost upon her hiding spot; he'd raised his lantern to scan the area, revealing his face. Restless eyes and dark hair were visible beneath a blood-red hood. Nasaru. This man's bearded mouth was moving as he searched. Was he… counting? The man – he might have been their leader based upon the golden wings sewn into his tunic – turned and gestured to her hiding place.

Two others joined him with blades drawn.

Mei's pulse quickened. Had they seen her? If she could circle around before they came too close… Her feet were stuck! Mei clenched her jaw as she tugged at her boots. One came free with a squelch.

The leader swung his lantern.

Mei tore at her other leg but the Nasaru was already circling around her cover. His eyes widened upon seeing her. Mei lashed out with her mind. The leader flew into the shadows, landing with a splat. His lantern had rolled away, but his voice rang out, issuing orders.

It had been a sharp attack but not her strongest; more of a reflex.

One of the Nasaru ran toward their fallen leader and Mei finally pulled her other foot free, only for darkness to snap down over her head. A musty fabric scent filled her nose. She ripped at the cloth, struggling with hands that caught her shoulders, but couldn't break the grip. Instead, she lashed out with another psychic blow.

Bone cracked and a man roared.

The sound turned her stomach and her heart thundered inside her chest, but she was free.

Mei flung the sack from her head. It was still dark, but at least the edges of lamplight offered some help.

She scrambled her way up and along the road, charging through shadows and heavy mist until her vision began to fail. Knives seemed to be slicing through her temples and her knees wobbled – far sooner than if she'd been attacked during the day. "No." She pleaded with her body, urging it on through force of will alone.

"Stop! We're not going to hurt you." The voice brought her to a halt. The words were strangely accented, but she understood most of them… didn't she? Either way, that did not mean the speaker could be trusted.

Mei collapsed to her knees.

Footsteps followed. When she lifted her head, breathing hard, three of the four men stood before her.

Two wore expressions of irritation. She recognised the leader in the third figure, covered as he was in mud. The missing one was probably the man who'd cried out. Hopefully, he was not too badly hurt.

*So long as he doesn't hold a grudge, I might survive…*

The muddy leader raised both hands, empty, in a show of

peace as he spoke again. "Please, *shi-ku*, we aren't trying to kill you."

Again, she understood most of what was said.

"Then leave me be." She pushed herself to her feet, holding her limbs rigid against the looming exhaustion. The soldiers seemed wary enough. Best to keep things that way... but she could not actually strike again.

"You are a long way from home," he said after a moment. Still, his accent did not sound quite right and not every word was clear. But generally, she understood. Was he speaking Senoja, then? "What are you doing in a place like this?"

"Travelling. Do not try and stop me, I don't want to hurt anyone else," she bluffed.

The Nasaru made no move and no sound. Mei stared at him. Was that a faint smile? Too hard to tell with the mud. Were they waiting for her to attack? Or collapse? Jeniva would have known what to do...

Something sharp pressed against her throat as an iron grip encircled her arm.

Mei stiffened. The cold sting of steel drew enough blood to trickle down her throat. The other soldier! The scent of his sweat was strong, the hard muscles of his chest against her shoulder like a wall.

"Careful now," the leader said. "Marhyn can be touchy. If you try to use your magic now, he might just cut your throat."

Mei remained still. She had no strength left to fight, and even if something *was* left, could she strike faster than the man's knife?

At a gesture from the leader, her captor undertook a quick search of her body. His hands were efficient as they lifted her father's knife from her belt, and then he walked her closer to the small group, his own weapon resting against the small of her back.

Was he the man whose arm she had broken?

In the light, Mei looked up at the leader next, who was busy wiping at the mud.

His face was unlined; he was not so many years her senior, and he smiled. It seemed a kind enough smile. Was it all part of some effort to keep her compliant as their prisoner? Even the simple gestures and words that sent two of his men to work on expanding her campsite were calm rather than forceful.

And yet a pressure emanated from him too; a pressure to listen, to obey.

She soon found herself sitting across from him in her own camp, resting on a slanted stone, whereas he stood. "So, you must tell me your name for I cannot call you 'little-one' forever."

"I am Mei." And that was all he needed to know, for now. But she kept her hands clenched together, beneath her knees, to stop them from shaking.

"My name is Anyo. I hope you will stay and talk with me tonight."

She frowned. "You haven't given me a choice."

"None, I admit. But you have my oath that we do not mean to kill you." He gestured to the rising flames from her fire, as one of his men continued to build it up – using dark, somewhat acrid pellets taken from a pack. "So please, enjoy the warmth of the fire and tell me what a young woman from Senoja is doing in the Malkaha Marsh?"

*****

For some reason, Anyo took time to make introductions.

The man called himself a 'Greyshield', though the others referred to him as 'Lord'. He was one of three who wore a close beard, but unlike the one called 'Han', Anyo's hair was not white.

Their armour and weapons were mismatched, leather and steel or sword and dagger, and their packs seemed to contain strange equipment and provisions like hammers, hooks and chisels, and food that seemed stored *within* other types of food. *Nothing like what Denuko carried.*

Anyo gestured the fourth of her captors, a man whose skin was not so dark as his own, nor was it at all pale like hers. "And over there is Marhyn, the man whose arm you broke before. He is from Cresideth in the north, a beastly place full of disgusting bugs and beautiful, dark-haired women with foul tempers."

Marhyn shook his head but did not respond, only taking out a small vial of black liquid, which he held up to the firelight to examine. His movements were not hampered at all... yet Anyo did not address the fact.

"He's been touchy since we entered the marsh," Anyo said to one of his companions, Katonga, who had an open face and was just as handsome as Anyo, now that she considered him. But Katonga only rolled his eyes at Anyo's words. The leader smiled and left the man to continue working on the meal, strips of white flesh swirling within a large pot.

The scent was a rich, savoury one but as a prisoner, would it even taste pleasant? "When will you release me?"

"That depends. Why are you here?"

Mei met his gaze. The story of being a healer was upon her lips but the people before her did not seem to be typical

Nasaru folk. Could she actually fool them? Mei hesitated. She'd already let them assume she was Senoja, but what was the best answer? For despite the warmth of the fire and the time to rest, she wasn't ready or possibly even *able* to blast her way out of the campsite.

Danger had not passed; it had only eased. "Collecting plants for medicine."

He glanced at her belt and pouches, which had already been searched. "Possibly. But I do not believe that is all."

She had no answer.

Anyo leant forward. "I cannot afford to spend all night interrogating you, and so I will make you an offer instead."

"What do you mean?"

Han was frowning but he did not speak.

"Simply that. Tell me the truth and if I believe you, you need not die."

A chill sliced through her body. *I can't lie my way out of this.* "If I do, how can I trust you?"

Anyo smiled. "You can only answer and see what happens – we both know your power is spent."

Mei glared at the man. "Then I don't have a choice."

He waited.

"I am searching for my brother. He is at least two days ahead of me."

Silence met her words.

"That is… not what I expected you to say."

"You might have encountered him, if you came from the north," she continued, not addressing his surprise. "He is far more powerful than I am, so if he was attacked, the destruction would be impossible to miss."

"Hmmm. And why are you not travelling together?"

"He was exiled," she said. "He's not worldly and so I followed him. That is the truth." There was no need to explain everything, no need to draw further attention to Iggy's unpreparedness for the Beyond – he was probably doing a better job than she. "Have you seen him?"

"No, we haven't, I'm sorry to say." Anyo rubbed at his chin as he regarded her. "Will you tell me what part of Senoja are you from? Your dialect is quite unfamiliar and even your clothing strikes me as a little old-fashioned."

"I am from Nokema."

"Nokema?" Anyo blinked. "Oh, you claim to be Inora."

"I *am* of the Inora."

Han spoke now, using the Nasaru tongue, only a few words.

Anyo raised a hand, but he nodded before directing another question at Mei. "And you came alone? Without your father or other family members to aid you in your search?"

"Our father is dead. I am the only one," Mei said, and found bitterness in her voice. The pressure she had felt earlier had not eased; there was something about the man, his expectation to be answered was so strong.

*He'd know if I lied.*

Even so, he couldn't possibly believe she was a spy – she'd be a poor excuse for one indeed, to be caught so easily.

Her captor conferred with Han, Katonga and Marhyn now, the Nasaru language somehow sharper or more decisive-sounding. When finally they stopped and Anyo addressed her again, tension had filled her limbs so much that an urge to lash out and release it was growing far too strong.

"I have to admit that I am at a loss, Mei. You appear to be

telling *something* resembling the truth, but my companions aren't sure." He raised the antique dagger. "On one hand, you carry a relic that appears to date to War of Tombs, something bearing the ancient symbols of Senoja nobility." Anyo gazed at her, his dark eyes curious. "And those pouches are also concerning."

"Medicines, as I said," Mei replied.

"Certainly. Only, you have enough snake-root to kill a giant, and enough *brightleaf* to raise a corpse."

"I need them for my search."

"So you claim. Yet you are equipped much as a *sun-killer*, or 'assassin' in my tongue. You are too dangerous to leave behind, and potentially too useful to kill, Mei. And so we will be taking you with us. You may even be able to help if you are innocent." He stood. "Later, if there is a later, we may turn you over to someone a little closer to King Mutolo."

"You think I am of the *Kel-ani*?" Mei asked. She could have laughed. *Kel-ani.* The title at least had been carried from the west to Nokema, all those years ago.

A secretive warrior-class from Senoja, trained in a wide variety of deadly arts, not the least of which was diplomacy; they were also called sun-killers, said to be so skilled as to commit their acts in broad daylight without being observed.

Anyo was not perturbed. "I have not discounted the possibility. When it comes to strangers from the west –"

Mei stood then and Anyo still towered over her. "I'm not from the west and my brother is in danger. I don't have time to go anywhere with you."

"Stay," he said quietly, his eyes hard now. "Have something to eat. You must be hungry since we interrupted your meal."

Katonga was already beside her, his blade pressed against

her side now, a sharp threat not yet piercing her tunic. She kept her fists clenched but did not make any sudden movement. "Please. Why would one of the *Kel-ani* allow herself to be captured this easily?"

"Sit, please," Anyo repeated his words, and despite the politeness, it was still a command. "You cannot help your brother if you force me to kill you."

Mei lowered herself to the ground and drew a shuddering breath, Katonga's blade remaining close. "And if you decide I'm a spy or assassin and imprison or kill me, how do I help him then?"

"Perhaps there is a third option."

"Being?"

"Tomorrow. But I will say this much now; your gifts may assist us in our endeavour."

Mei glared at the campfire a moment, before lifting her gaze to her captor. "Fine."

"That is what I had hoped to hear." He bent to the fire then and scooped some of the boiled meat into a bowl, crouching beside her and handing it over. "But let me give you a final warning. When you recover, should you try to attack one of us, you will have no less than three knives in your torso the very moment you do."

She accepted the food with a frown.

# CHAPTER 24. – MEI

Mei followed Anyo beneath a clear sky, the others never far behind, even as they took turns scouting the marsh. Warmth from the sun's rays sank into her skin and bones, adding a sense of simmering power to her movements.

A welcome contrast to last night.

Especially after being held in the grip of mist for so long prior. Her body seemed almost impatient to move, to strike, but with the sunlight came a new kind of insect; a small, jumping bug of red that leapt from nearby shrubs and onto exposed skin. Not yet noon, she was covered in itching bites.

A trial of endurance with her hands bound.

The only way to put the irritations from her mind was to focus on escape.

At the least, it was still possible to navigate bogs and sink holes while bound, to follow Anyo's steps along the smaller trails, as she ran over her dwindling set of options.

Little had changed in the time since her capture.

The men were still heading deep into the marsh, somehow finding solid ground in a maze of murky pools, deep green channels and clumps of unstable islands – different to the edges she'd travelled before.

Her captors managed the feat by using a series of long poles cut from the edge of the road, though Anyo seemed to rely on something else too, a small object held in his hand. Mei guessed that her only chance of returning to the road was to gain possession of it – otherwise she would become lost all too quickly. Just a single misstep and she'd risk drowning.

Freeing her hands was another stumbling block, along with overpowering four well-trained men; one whom followed her and whose eyes she felt on her back... *and* she had to do it all without blacking out from overuse of her power.

While it seemed her psychic strength was as strong or stronger than it had been since she left the Valley, was that really enough? Even with some sort of catalyst, something unexpected, to give her a chance to lash out, even if it was something the men weren't ready for... could she really escape? More, one of them was a sorcerer – Marhyn, who had recovered so quickly from her attack.

Above all her concerns remained the location. *If* she escaped, to where would she flee? And how could she find Iggy while being pursued by Anyo?

The so-called lord brought their small party to a halt in a modest clearing so they could eat the midday meal. He waved at the insects as he did, muttering under his breath. Mei found a relatively dry log and sat.

Rotten timber creaked, and she fell into the hollow trunk as it broke.

Hands bound, she struggled to right herself.

"Let me help." Anyo grabbed her tied hands and pulled her up, his face set in a wide smile.

Mei didn't thank him, but accepted the bread he handed her a moment later. Han, also called Hanibalo at times, was searching the clearing for something, kicking at clumps of grass and wiping moss from the ground, his face intent. Katonga crouched by the water's edge, a thin line trailing in the green channel.

Marhyn ate in silence and Anyo did so too, only he watched her.

"How do you speak my language so well?" Mei eventually asked.

"I learnt it during my time as a soldier, and before that, as a diplomatic envoy for the king himself. I actually spent a year in the Senoja Emperor's own household."

Hanibalo snickered from the other side of the clearing and Katonga glanced over his shoulder. "Diplomatic envoy? That's a new one."

Anyo glared at the man, throwing a crust into the grass. "That's right, Katonga. An *envoy*. For the king himself."

"Whatever you say, *Lord Anyo*."

Mei watched the men chuckling amongst themselves, as if they carried hardly a care in the world. And maybe they didn't. It all seemed good-natured enough. No doubt it would be too much to ask for them to be driven apart by some secret rift.

Although, of all her captors, Marhyn did not join in.

Anyo travelled with men he had obviously known for some time to complete an unknown task in a distant marsh full of nothing but bugs and dampness. Something that Anyo claimed she could help with. Marhyn was the exception to the easy mood. Standoffish and not quite part of the general camaraderie.

"Marhyn, I have something." Hanibalo was waving from the centre of the clearing. Mei followed to where the older man was bent over a nest. It rose from a pile of weeds, grey and green moss covering the sides. Hanibalo's deep voice bore some traces of excitement and he looked up at the Cresidethian. "What do you think? Steep slope. Three openings."

Marhyn grunted as he knelt to examine the nest. Hanibalo stared at the fellow a moment, then switched back the sharper sounds of his native tongue, and the two began to discuss the heap... most likely, at least.

"What's happening?" Mei asked Anyo.

The man answered without taking his eyes from the nest. "Han may have found a clue to our goal. If this is the nest of the swamp-ant, the striped swamp-ant, to be precise, then we may have reached our destination."

Not much of an answer. "And where is that?"

Anyo raised a hand for her to wait while he spoke with Marhyn, who was shaking his head. After a few moments of pointing and further discussion, they returned to their packs and set off again. Instead of leading, Anyo handed Marhyn the object Mei noticed earlier, letting the quiet man guide them, and kept pace with Mei.

"What did you just give him?"

"Something from a sorcerer, so I can't explain how it works myself, but it helps us stay on firm ground."

"And what do ants have to do with this? With whatever you're here for?"

"Can't you tell by now?"

"How could I?" Mei asked. "You haven't said anything."

"Then let me tell you a tale while we walk," he said, and his face was lit from within by a hunger she hadn't seen before. It infused his words and Mei found herself listening closely. "A mere handful of years before the War of Tombs, one of the Seven Princes of Omaila left the palace in a rage, having argued with his father. Rinbe was said to be so furious with the king that he drew his sword and challenged his father to a duel – using his free hand to hold back his weeping mother. Perhaps an exaggeration fit for a melodrama, but who can say?"

"So, this is a myth?"

"That is what we're here to discover."

"But, how?"

"Let me finish, and you will see," he said with a smile. "Now, no blows were exchanged but the youngest prince renounced his title and his wealth. As the youngest son of seven, he was in no real danger of having to take the throne but the people of Nasaru loved him. Of what history has survived, it *is* written that Rinbe was a kind and generous young man, often stopping in the street to help men with their work, to listen to the troubles of the elderly or play with children. He is said to have once rescued a fisherman's son from a wharf, diving into rough seas and dragging the boy to the shore."

"What drove him away?" Mei said. "It sounds like his life was blessed."

"Can you guess?"

"It's your story."

Anyo shrugged. "The bitterness of love, of course. He had fallen for a baker's daughter; a happy girl with a well-to do family, yes, but not someone of noble birth."

"And that matters in your nation?"

"To some," he said.

Mei frowned.

"Yet it was worse, for she had been born with Senoja blood in her veins and thus Misha was totally unacceptable to the king."

"I see," Mei said. "The king was a coward who could not accept his son's choice."

"Perhaps. But the Senoja had sent an assassin to poison his only daughter just months before, and so his grudge was not so simple."

"Oh."

"But Rinbe did not care; for why should one suffer for a political choice made by rulers on the other side of the world? He and Misha had a love that welled up within them and brought even those nearby such joy that it was said the great God Aehtu smiled upon them. Rinbe had wrongly hoped that as youngest, his choices would have little effect on the Royal Family."

Hanibalo glanced over his shoulder, expression hard to read. Was it one of fondness… or sadness, perhaps?

Mei looked back to Anyo. It was an odd contrast that the man seemed so passionate about the tale. "So, he fled after confronting his father?"

"Yes. Stealing away one night, he took Misha and slipped into the southern plains, pursued by his brothers. Days and weeks passed, with Rinbe sometimes staying just a matter of hours ahead of his family. Whether they meant to bring him home in chains with an apology or to take his head, none know. But when they finally did reach him, after a long and torturous flight of weeks, Rinbe and Misha had reached the edges of the Malkaha Marsh."

"Here? Are you searching for their graves then?"

Anyo shook his head as he swatted at a pair of the horrible insects. "Not quite. But let me finish the tragic tale. Rinbe had travelled far and wide across Nasaru for peace but had never shaken off his brothers. Now, they faced him from their mounts, a ragged and exhausted man, his horse long dead and his body sick with hunger. Misha stood by him, her good-natured face determined as ever.

"The eldest prince dismounted, gaunt and exhausted too. 'Come home now, little brother,' he said. 'We miss you, as do Mother and Father. It is our dearest wish that you be happy again.' Rinbe responded with hope. 'Truly, brother? But then, why have you chased us so mercilessly, if we were always welcome?' The older man glanced at his siblings before sighing. 'While we want your happiness, it will not be with this Senoja harlot.'

"Upon hearing such words, Rinbe tore his blade free. 'Do not say that again, brother of mine'. The older prince drew his own sword. 'Rinbe, she is not for you! A half-breed, and Senoja to boot! A prince must never sully himself with such a whore.'

"Rinbe's knuckles where white. 'No, brother. You stain yourself with such words.' The older prince ground his teeth. 'Do I, Rinbe?'"

Mei found herself leaning closer. "And then what?"

"Those were the last words he said. Rinbe streaked forward and with a single blow, took off his brother's head. His siblings were dumbfounded. Rinbe shouted for all to leave, to never return but one reached for his blade and so he, too, died. By now the remaining princes leapt into battle, but to no avail

– all were slain by Rinbe's hand, his fury and his skill simply too great. Afterwards he wept, inconsolable, but eventually Misha's gentle remonstrations calmed him, and together they collected the bodies of his family and dragged them into the Malkaha Marsh. There they built cairns and disappeared, never to be seen again by the king or queen, by the Royal Sentinels or by any who searched after."

Mei was silent a moment when he finished speaking. "But if no-one saw them again, and all the brothers died, how do you know so much of what happened?"

"I asked the same question of my instructor when she told me the tale."

"And?"

"Misha herself left the Marsh to tell of Rinbe's death not ten years later. She shared her tale with a farmer on the plain before dying herself that very night – if you believe the some of the more popular stories, though they are many and varied."

Mei looked around the mostly flat, sparsely-covered swamp. "So, you want to find Rinbe's grave?"

He nodded. "And his sword."

"Why?"

Katonga chuckled from ahead. "You left that part out again, Anyo."

The man frowned. "People tend to get the wrong idea when I don't."

From nearby, though he did not turn his head from where he searched the marsh, Han snorted. "You probably shouldn't tell that tale anymore, lad. Especially not to someone who doesn't need to hear it."

"She may prove useful, you know."

"What's he talking about?" Mei asked with a frown, this time directed at Han.

"I did leave out an important detail. Rinbe's sword is a Royal Heirloom, handed down from a line of Nasaru Kings that date back before our arrival here two thousand years ago. Supposedly," he added, and once more his eyes grew fierce with desire. "It is also said to be a weapon of significant power, called *Sothalic* or 'Mirror-stone' in the old Nasaru tongue. It has powers unseen in centuries."

"I see," Mei said, and the truth was... disappointing. But then, what had she expected? True nobility? And to learn that simple greed or lust for power was his motivation did not fill her with hope for the future.

Anyo stopped. "Make no mistake, it is one of the most priceless things in all the lands, and when I find it, I will change those lands for the better."

His claim was not reassuring. "And what does this have to do with me?"

"As I have said, I want you to help us."

"Then promise to set me free after," Mei said. "Then I'll help you." Was that something Jeniva would have said? Jeniva would have stood taller while she made a demand. Mei straightened, her jaw set. "Well, Anyo? Give me your answer."

He smiled. "Oh?"

Mei hesitated. He was not intimidated at all, and she resisted the urge to take a step back. "You wouldn't have brought me this far if you didn't need me."

The bearded man held her gaze a moment longer before raising an eyebrow. "You would do much for this brother of yours, wouldn't you?"

"Yes."

His face hardened. "Then let me remind you that you are already helping me, in exchange for your life. Now let us quicken our step."

***

Another night spent battling the insects for sleep was passing and Mei found herself close to screaming – there seemed zero possibility that she'd ever be still again. "Like a bloody windmill," she muttered at one point, spinning her arms to swat at gnats or to rub at the bites.

At least she was no longer bound.

But escape still seemed impossible. Even if she could steal the guiding stone, could she gather enough supplies without being seen? And that left the marsh itself; could she escape it, let alone outrun her captors?

Each time she woke, temptation caused her limbs to twitch.

She rolled onto her side. Marhyn stood on watch somewhere beyond the firelight but Anyo lay close to the feeble flames, his face tilted into shadow. Was he even asleep? Was trusting him a mistake? Once he had his sword, there was every chance he'd simply hand her over to his king as a spy.

Or worse.

And there were still the vague answers given for her purpose. Exactly *how* did they think she could help? Finding Rinbe was not something she could do, even with her psychic abilities. Yet one thing seemed clear. A wave of expectation flowed from across the camp – from Anyo. Was he awake after all? Waiting for her to attempt escape? Was untying her some sort of trap? To prove one way or another if she was a Senoja spy?

She glared but it was impossible to tell whether he was awake, not based on the gentle rise and fall of his chest. Her gifts were rarely wrong. If such a strong sense of purpose or desire poured forth from another person, then it could usually be trusted.

Anyo *wanted* her to attempt escape.

He had not lowered his guard at all. It was a test.

*I can wait for the right moment.*

CHAPTER 25. – MEI

Mei watched Marhyn gesture where everyone crowded around another half-concealed nest. Unlike the previous nest, this peak had been built atop a low wall of earth and it lay beneath two ferns near as tall as the men themselves. More pleasant sunshine fell upon Mei's back as she watched the man explain… something in Nasaru.

A change had come across the swamp. Three days travel and now solid ground was more frequent, and there were even small hills. More, everything seemed cleaner. Water streaming down from distant mountains was clearer too, having spent less time spreading into channels and mingling with the dirt and moss.

Even the blasted biting gnats had lessened in number.

*Iggy might have taken this very same path.*

Probably a vain hope, but all she really had.

More changes were obvious; some of the shrubs bore little orange flowers shaped as spirals, and every now and then fair-sized trees thrust up from the earth, their golden brown leaves and mottled trunks seeming to be a feature rather than sign of malaise.

And finally, Katonga and Hanibalo used their probing staves less and less, while Anyo rarely took out the guiding stone.

Instead, they followed Marhyn from nest to nest. Only once had Mei seen a yellow swamp-ant itself, a large insect with broad, shiny wings. It swooped over from the water and slipped into a patch of trees. Almost before she saw it, Marhyn was running after the ant, tracking it to the low wall where they now stood.

"Why are they so important?" she asked Anyo as she paused to catch her breath.

"Misha told the farmer that she and Rinbe followed the ants to a place of great beauty within the marsh. The striped ants especially like to feast on the sweet flowers that grow there, or so Marhyn suspects, and thus the more yellow ants we come across, the closer we are to Rinbe and Misha's haven. More so the striped, yellow ant."

"How can you be sure?"

"We cannot. But the trail must be followed to the end."

So, on they searched, stopping only for water and a rushed meal of a hard, flat bread, their pace increasing as they discovered more and more nests.

Anyo's eyes grew brighter with each discovery, and leading them on faster each time. Mei found herself struggling to keep up with the increased speed. There were more wildflowers of yellow, white and scarlet now, and she saw another family of otters upon the banks of one channel. The animals scattered as the men ran on, trampling moss and grass.

She nearly asked for a break but a call from ahead stopped her. Marhyn was no-where in sight and Anyo had bent to examine another tree trunk, where a fresh mark had been slashed into the bark.

"What's happening?" she asked Hanibalo.

"Marhyn is tracking the ants but when they fly, he can't afford to wait for us, so he marks the trees. That way we don't lose him." He shook his head. "Never seen someone move that fast. Like he's part dragonfly."

The ant's trail turned back toward the dark smudges of mountains in the distance. All around, trees grew thicker as the trail rose and dipped, leading them across streams and around deep pools. Once again, Mei was struck by just how different this part of the marsh was – far clearer and cleaner.

Anyo led them up a steady rise that seemed to stretch endlessly and when at last they crested it, Mei set her back against the bark of the nearest tree and closed her eyes. The sun had slipped behind cloud covering, and a chill settled into the air – or maybe it was just her sweat cooling.

Anyo drew in a breath, clutching her arm. "Rinbe's Valley."

She flinched at the unexpected touch, but the man was already moving again.

Katonga smacked a fist into his palm. "By Aehtu, we'd never have found this without Marhyn or the ants. Or that sorcerer's carving."

"Indeed, old friend."

Down the slope the trees thinned to reveal a broad, green meadow with a deep depression in the centre. The valley was lined with more red and golden wildflowers, white ones too, and smooth rocks along with others streaked by sparkling granite.

A peace absent from the rest of the marsh hung over the small valley.

Even the last of the red, jumping insects were gone. *Finally.*

Farther below, somewhat obscured by Anyo who continued his slow, almost reverent descent, a grove of fir trees rose from the centre of the depression. They cast cool shadows across a structure in their centre, details vague. Surely, it was Rinbe's home?

The sun peeked from the clouds again, brightening the meadow and sparkling on dew... no, upon the yellow ants, their wings fluttering as they rose from the flowers. Bees were mixed in with the ants, their buzzing faint.

Mei caught up with Anyo.

He spoke over his shoulder. "On to Rinbe's refuge then, everyone. I do not know what we will find within. Be ready."

"Wait," Mei said. "Tell me how I am supposed to help. What are we going to find here? And where is Marhyn?"

Hanibalo and Katonga were working on lamps and Anyo now drew his sword, which he used to point to the structure. "Inside, I imagine."

"He couldn't wait for us?"

"No, he couldn't," he said. "Marhyn always meant to betray us, but that's where you will earn your freedom, Mei. Protect us if you can. He is more than he looks."

She stared.

"I am not lying, if that's what you're thinking."

"No... I don't..." She shook her head. "Why? And how is he different?"

"He is a sorcerer, of course." Anyo shrugged. "But he was a necessary tool. And as for why, he wants what we want."

She folded her arms. "So, you expect me to kill him?"

He stopped. "One of us may have to. But I doubt that your skills are limited to violence. Your Senoja heritage offers more than that, yes? You will sense him."

"I am Inora."

"So you say," Anyo replied as he resumed walking. "Stay close."

Mei followed him down to the structure. A large dwelling with a low roof, it spread across the land rather than climbing up for multiple storeys. Its stones had obviously been carved with care, considering the condition it was in, even half-covered in leaves.

Had there once been a door or had it long-since rotted away?

Was Marhyn lurking beyond? Ready to strike? He was a sorcerer, which meant he could speak fire or cast ice into her bones, like in the stories… didn't it? *Or maybe something worse.*

Mei kept a hold on her gift, letting her senses expand.

A bird cry rang out.

She jumped, glancing back at the meadow. Overhead, clouds were creeping toward the sun, stretching forth like ghostly fingers.

"Come, Mei," Anyo called from within the building.

# CHAPTER 26. – ROKURA

Deep shadows cloaked Rokura as he crept along cold tiles of the rooftop, hidden by not only his black clothing but the clouds that covered up the night sky, with only faint starlight managing to sneak free.

Soldiers patrolling the walls watched the mountain pass, and guards upon the barracks' grounds were few enough during peace-time, posing no obstacle for Rokura, who had simply to exercise patience.

While he waited for footfalls below to fade, he crouched still, breathing slow and easy, reviewing his path. First the window on the storage attic, and the passage with its heavy runners patterned as mountain peaks, and then Conisz' meeting room below and finally the ledger. Even in the dark, the meeting room lock could be picked; standard Nasaru military construction, and within a small pouch on his belt, a fragment of soft charcoal for the ledger.

Without access to the window, there was servant's entrance and the kitchens, which were soon to awaken to begin their often-thankless work, much of it before dawn.

Rokura crept onward, placing each hand and foot carefully,

checking for any sense of movement before coming to a halt at the scaffold. A perfectly functional ladder that granted access the window appeared as planned – such convenient repairs granting him quite a boon.

Something that would not have been in place during wartime.

He drew a dagger and set to work, moving swiftly as he dug into the old wood of the frame until he was, after some time, at last able to pull the whole thing free from the wall, setting it down carefully.

Then, he parted the curtains with the point of his blade and waited.

No sounds from within.

A good sign but not a conclusive one.

He parted them further and peered into the darkness. Still no sense of anyone in the room; time to move. Rokura climbed from the sill to land inside softly, slipping into a crouch where he listened once more.

Nothing. There was a vague sense of boxes or perhaps covered furniture that seemed to be arranged neatly.

He removed a small glow-stone of Black Coral, faint light offering enough for him to navigate the room and pause at the door to listen. With no sounds below, he turned the handle and entered the dark corridor, moving across the runner to the stairs and finding himself before the meeting room in moments.

He knelt before the lock, placing the glow-stone in his mouth as he removed the thin tools he needed. The carved Coral still offered his tongue the faint taste of salt as he worked.

The lock soon clicked free and he gathered his tools to slip into the room. There, Rokura opened the cabinet, removed the ledger and carried it to the table where he paused to listen once more. Once again, he was alone.

Rokura set the glow-stone down. "Let's see what you are hiding," he whispered.

On the most recent page was a list of sanctioned merchants, a few travellers, small troop movements, but no large groups. Yet of most interest was the next, blank page – when he ran his fingertips across the surface, he found faint indentations of writing. Rokura lifted a piece of charcoal and rubbed it across the page, revealing the impression of words and numbers.

Many were unfinished due to uneven writing pressure but halfway down the page, the final entry showed the word 'orders' clearly and then 'Bed' and what might have been the beginning of an 'o' right after...

Duke Bedoa?

Rokura replaced the charcoal with a frown. It could have been a different name... Yet who else would give orders that could bind a local governor? Only the king, and that was not at all likely. Just as concerning, exactly what orders had been issued? Who had passed the border? The disc was unerring; it still showed the rebels south...

*Treachery is afoot.*

He carefully tore the page free, brushed the traces of char away and returned the ledger to its place in the cabinet. Finally, it was time to leave, to set the window back in place and return to his room.

Where he would get little sleep.

If Bedoa *was* involved it might be no surprise, considering his vocal disagreements with many of the king's decisions... but no gain could come from leaping to that conclusion, or to any conclusion. Governor Conisz would have to be questioned. Or at least, investigated further. If the fellow was an unwilling pawn, that was one thing, but if he was involved more deeply, then his life was forfeit.

As was Bedoa's.

***

But when the morning sun broke through the open curtains and Rokura rose to prepare for the day and seek the governor, the man was not to be found – his aide explaining that Conisz had left for the surrounding villages to enforce the collection of taxes.

More, Lettaka and his men had arrived when Rokura made his way to the stables, ready to begin the search of the ravine. The prospect of finding answers seemed little to grow excited over – with so many young prisoners, it was extremely unlikely the rebels would have been able to make them climb down into the mountain, if Lettaka's description was correct.

And there was no reason to doubt the man.

No reason to visit the ravine, either.

Instead, it was better to send a message to King Mutolo, and then resume his chase – for the deeper the rebels travelled toward Takirov, the harder they would become to find, let alone intercept. "Prime Scout Lettaka, we'll be travelling the highway south."

Lettaka paused, one hand on his saddle. "Of course, if you are certain, My Lord."

He smiled. "Are you certain no-one has passed near the city, and that there is only one path through to Takirov, beyond the punishing detours we discussed yesterday?"

"I am," he replied without a hint of hesitation.

"Then that leaves only one path." He lifted the wooden disc. "This tells me my quarry is south of here, which in turn tells me they took the highway."

"But... wouldn't that mean they deceived the commander at the border?" one of the other scouts asked, a short fellow who seemed weary, judging by the rings beneath his eyes.

"Possibly."

"Or they had help," Lettaka suggested, expression darkening.

The other man frowned. "But who would do that?"

"Everyone has a price, Udoc."

"Well, it's still hard to believe."

Rokura swung into his saddle. Another question that had no answer... though betrayal didn't sound like something cousin Cosequ would be a party to. "Let's see if we can find the truth."

Beyond the city, the climb up into the grey mountain range was slow at first, and when they stopped to water their mounts, Rokura was sure to give Arrow some extra care. While the stony highway started steep, it eventually levelled out some, winding around barren ravines, slipping within the shadows of the peaks. A small reward of rock-carvings was revealed – images of battles cut deep into the stone, figures with long spears riding large beasts that bore wings.

The mythical dragon-riders of the Ancients.

Yet so few bones or other evidence had been found that it was hard to believe in such creatures.

The journey to the command post was not so long that another rest was needed, but he'd found himself counting roadside markers, impatience growing inside him as he stared across at fortified buildings of dark stone.

They overlooked a sharp dip in the highway, sides of the road boasting tree-stumps and bare stones, providing as little cover as possible for the approach. Rumours he was yet to confirm suggested that stretches of road were set to collapse in the case of a serious attack from Takirov, but it had always seemed fanciful. No-one in Nasaru wanted goods to stop flowing between the nations. Especially not the Black Coral.

Such a difficult and costly measure would probably not have been taken, but the two score of soldiers and their small catapults, archers and battle sorcerers with their burning coral would hold off any vanguard long enough to light the beacons and warn the garrison in Mamoya.

Of more concern remained the truth of the betrayal.

Had Duke Bedoa – or someone else – planted traitors within Mamoya, within the post? Unlikely that only a handful could manage to conceal Brutan and his prisoners as they passed through. And equally unlikely was the notion the entire post was now made up of traitors – even Cosequ?

Surely not.

Would it all make sense if Bedoa's motives were clear? He was a malcontent, a greedy worm to boot, but neither quality equalled treason... at least, not alone. Not without more than a suspicion and a missing page, not without proof.

A tall figure exited the command post, hailing them as he did. "Welcome back to the real border, Lord Rokura."

Captain Cosequ was an older breed of Battle Sorcerer, wearing breastplate and armour, unlike other sorcerers. A long braid fell free when he removed his burnished helm with its engraved crest of Royal Wings.

"I hope for a pleasant visit, Cosequ," he replied. "Are you

well? Are the mountains quiet?"

"They have little to share, gladly," he replied with a grin. "Join me inside, I am eager to learn what brings you here, cousin."

Rokura left Lettaka to care for the mounts and joined the captain in an austere room, decorated only with a fruit bowl bearing red apples and a single war trophy upon the wall – a monstrous greatsword of the Ministo; warriors from centuries lost, its obsidian form somehow stronger than steel and certainly too heavy to wield.

After Rokura summarised what he had learnt and what he suspected, Cosequ glared out the window. "I do not like this."

"Nor I."

The man stood and then took an apple from the bowl, gripping it hard enough to turn his knuckles white. Then he smashed it against the stone wall. Juice ran down the stone. "If someone has truly hoodwinked me in such a way..."

Had it not been so serious, Rokura might have smiled. Cosequ thrived on the dramatic at times, and his pride was quite considerable, but a kingdom could fall if the rebels had truly smuggled Asaro Itonye out of the nation.

And if not, the lives of innocent people were still at stake.

"Then you'll assist us."

He nodded. "I will indeed. And I believe I know exactly where to start looking. Not only that, I'm sure it will marry up with the impressive wooden disc you have."

"Oh?"

"If anyone was brave, or mad enough to sneak through the border here, they would take two paths. One, farther along the highway, believing in the strength of their deception to deceive even the Beholders in Takirov."

"And is that possible?"

Cosequ shrugged. "I doubt as much. They know their way around the Black Coral as well as we do."

"It's likely that they have something to assist them – they have not been detected here."

"Or they were assisted by someone here, which I will investigate, believe me."

"Then the second path?"

The Battle Sorcerer returned to his seat and wiped his hands upon his pant legs with a toothy grin. "The ruins of Vi Mekadymu."

Rokura glanced over at the greatsword on the wall. Cosequ spoke of more history – Vi Mekadymu, the melting city hidden within the nearby mountains. An ancient bastion of a lost people known only as the False Ones.

A dread place.

One that did indeed speak to the bravery or foolishness of the rebels.

Few that ventured within returned, and those that did would speak little, if at all, of whatever they had witnessed. Most current Nasaru knowledge of the ruin came from a single sorcerer who returned possessed of dark mood swings and a habit of slipping into an unknown tongue at uncertain times.

If the Takirov had already entered such a place, it was too late. Unless they carried some secret protection.

"We can probably confirm their path with your trinket."

"At the very least, we must do that much," Rokura said with a nod.

Cosequ smacked a fist into his palm. "That's the spirit. We'll start with the ruins."

"Are you that keen to risk your life?"

"It's more about showing them they cannot get away with pulling the wool over my eyes, cousin."

## CHAPTER 27. – MEI

The ancient home of Prince Rinbe stood thick with lichen and cobwebs. Thin, high windows let watery light into the room, spreading across the stone floor to run up the opposite wall, drawing Mei's gaze to the skeleton of a cabinet, one broken door ajar.

Fragments of what may have been cloth or parchment rested on shelves, she could not tell. A stone fireplace faced the entryway and in it lay a blackened heap of steel, but no other furniture.

Other rooms were but darkened shadows.

Anyo knelt by the fireplace while Hanibalo and Katonga examined the walls and floor. Searching for signs of Marhyn? Mei drifted toward the arch beside the fireplace, looking deeper into the dark house. Without windows in the other rooms, she could see little, only vague shapes of furniture and other doorways.

"Mei, can you read this?" Anyo beckoned and she knelt beside him.

He held a steel plaque, its edges fire-blackened. Mei took a single glance at the symbols and shook her head. "It's too old."

And it was probably true – but she could not read it no matter the age. The symbols were similar to what she used for writing back home, but not the same.

"No matter," he said, and glanced away, and it seemed he was counting beneath his breath again.

Mei had no time to wonder at his behaviour, as Hanibalo's deep voice boomed from somewhere in the house. "Anyo, there's a trapdoor leading underground."

"Yes, of course there is," Anyo whispered, and Mei stared after him as he strode to the next room and Hanibalo's light.

The man knew more than he was letting on.

She did not follow at once. Was this the time to escape? While Anyo was so obviously distracted?

Katonga nudged her after his leader.

Not a good time after all.

The lanterns cast shadows across Rinbe's kitchen. The room contained a three-legged stove and a basin beneath the windows, these filled with a mixture of rubble and branches. Pale lichen spread in patterns, almost like faces trapped within the walls.

Faces that were straining toward her.

Or so it seemed.

She shivered. Was the room trying to tell her something? *That's never happened before.* Her gifts were definitely *not* only connected to violence, true enough. But such a vision – if her eyes had not been playing tricks – was new.

The feeling passed and she did not mention it. The threat of Marhyn was more important.

"The roof has fallen in there," Anyo said, as he led Mei into the next room without pausing. There, they found two bed frames, one large and one small. At the far end of the room, Hanibalo stood over an open hatch, its steel lid resting on the floor.

"Marhyn?" Anyo asked.

"Seems likely," the white-haired man replied as he gestured. "Look at this. Scrape marks on the floor. The lid has been opened recently." He glanced at Katonga. "To be certain, check the back of the house."

"Right." The man turned back along the passage.

"Let's wait a moment then," Anyo said as he began to pace, lantern swinging.

Mei felt her chest tighten. Was Marhyn waiting below? Damn him. *What* was below? If she extended her senses now, assuming he was close by, she'd succeed. After all, sensing the power of a sorcerer would not be so different to sensing Iggy's gifts, or the gifts of anyone from the village, for that matter... surely?

"I'll seek him," Mei said.

Anyo nodded. "Good."

Mei closed her eyes let her awareness slide down beneath the floor, passing through the chill of the stone and earth, the age of it almost something she could taste – a disconcerting experience, and once more, not something that had happened in the past.

She found a wide, empty space, a darkness.

But somewhere below came a shimmering so persistent that it stung her mind. She clenched her jaw and sought it, drifting down a narrow passage to where a modest, circular room waited.

And in the centre, a stone casket rested beneath a shrine

that was indistinct.

But detail of the carven figure upon the casket was clear – a strikingly handsome man with a beard and a sad smile. The hum of power from within blocked her from sensing anything else... yet it was almost like an echo. A powerful one, but an echo only.

If anyone did wait below, all hints of them were buried by whatever rested inside the casket.

*Sothalic?*

"Anything?" Anyo asked.

Mei opened her eyes, vision fading. Katonga had returned, and he waited beside Hanibalo, apparently having discovered nothing.

"There's a casket down there, in a circular room at the end of a long corridor. A man's likeness is carved upon it and it seems like something powerful lies within. Or once did, I can't be sure. I think it's blocking me from sensing much else."

"The prince? A crowned man with a beard?"

"He was bearded but no crown."

"Of course," Anyo said, shaking his head and continuing, almost to himself. "Why would he have a crown, having renounced his title?"

"We might have found something at last, lad," Hanibalo said with a grin.

"So I hope," Anyo replied with a smile of his own. "I will go first."

He lowered his lantern into the opening. A series of rungs formed a ladder that led down to the earth. Mei stood over him as he descended, probing the dark with her mind still, but she found nothing beyond the sense of what seemed to be the *Sothalic*.

"You next," Hanibalo said.

Mei hesitated a moment, then stepped down, her skin flinching at the cold iron when her hands wrapped around the first rung.

But she descended and no attack came.

At the bottom, Anyo was tapping his foot while the others climbed. "There is only one way," he said the moment they were all gathered, then took them along the narrow passage.

The walls were rough-hewn and the floor uneven. A longer walk to reach the room than Mei expected, even having seen it in her mind. And still she took every step expecting Marhyn to leap from the darkness ahead.

But nothing and no-one did.

When they reached the chamber, the shrine was finally revealed in detail – a large hawk, its wingspan broader than a regular hawk. And beneath the shrine was a large dais, dominated entirely by the stone casket.

It, too, looked made by hands accustomed to working with stone. The statue was simple but captured a likeness of the prince. Rinbe's face had been carved with more care than the rest of him. Had another hand had worked at it also? Little more than an impression, perhaps if she touched it would she know? *Unlikely, even with everything else that has happened in this strange place.*

Anyo placed his lantern in a hollow which looked to have been made for such a purpose, then stepped onto the dais. Silence was heavy beneath the ground, as was a dampness to the air. She did not want to break the hush. No-one else spoke either, Hanibalo and Katonga appeared to be holding their breath.

And still no Marhyn.

The sorcerer had to be hiding in the house or valley above. The shrine was too small, and with four people within there was little room to move, so where was the man? And why was Anyo no longer concerned?

The lord or Greyshield leant over the casket and reached out to take the shoulders of the statue, bowing his head. He remained still for long moments.

Not the actions of a greedy treasure hunter at all. Anyo's next movements were equally reverent as he straightened, then knelt to lay his blade at Rinbe's feet.

He rested his fingertips on the lid then.

"Time to claim my heritage."

# CHAPTER 28. – ROKURA

Cosequ led the way from the command post as warm sunlight slipped between the jagged ridges, columns and peaks, grey stone dark where it climbed above them like a torn curtain. It was only the eastern side of the range that let sunlight spear through to cast long stripes of light across the broad road.

To the west, the mountain rose, covered in a sea of trees, dark in the stillness of morning save for slashes of green where the sunlight reached their leaves. If one were to tunnel directly west, they would reach the city of Pemmka, but further east and south, where the trail led, waited the ruins of Vi Mekadymu. And if there *was* a safe path through the mountain, then the exit point may well be deep within the Black Coral Reefs.

The Reefs were hardly a viable refuge for a rebel stronghold, considering how heavily regulated they were. *Were Brutan, and possibly the duke himself, seeking a ship?* A troubling thought, since it would suggest a much larger group of traitors.

"What do they know that we do not?" Rokura murmured, reins held loosely in one hand.

"My Lord?" Lettaka spoke from nearby, Udoc and his other men riding closer to Cosequ, keeping a close watch on the road and surroundings. For the moment, the magical disc confirmed the rebel's passage but once Cosequ took them off the highway, confirmation of physical signs of passage would be welcome.

"It's nothing," Rokura replied with a wave of his hand. "Just thinking to myself."

Yet his doubts could not be waved away so easily. They clung to him until mid-morning, when Cosequ turned into a low depression half-screened by shrubs spotted with flowers. The depression led to a broken, overgrown road that swung around a horseshoe-shaped gorge. Its sides were steep, with piles of stone and faded tree trunks, evidence of old slides. The distant bottom promised a cruel but swift death upon yet more rock formations.

"Not much of a road now, is it?" Cosequ called from where he led them, with only room for two horses abreast now.

"How long until we reach the ruin?"

"Not long at all. The outskirts can be found around the next bend," he replied. "It's just a few stumps of an outpost, really."

Some of the columns that towered above were still crumbling, as suggested by a recent jumble of stones that littered the road ahead. It was not enough to block their passage but picking a way through slowed the horses and would have hampered chained prisoners.

"Any sign of their passage?" Rokura asked Lettaka. The prime scout had leaned over in his saddle, then dismounted to examine the slide.

He nodded. "A few fresh scratches. I think the larger piece at the start of the slide was moved recently too."

"They might now be travelling with a sorcerer," Rokura said.

"Certainly likely, My Lord."

Once free of the mess, Cosequ picked up the pace again and they soon reached a great stair leading up and off the road. It climbed beneath more sheer walls of grey stone, steps broad yet shallow. The centre bore furrows of several sizes for carts that no longer travelled the mountain.

The base of the stair revealed rectangular walls hardly higher than the fetlocks of their horses. *The ruined outpost.* Hardy, yellowed weeds clung to life in the gaps and inside, not a single scrap of wood or metal.

But there were messages upon the stone face of the stair.

One had been chiselled in, hard edges worn down by wind and water. It simply read: 'Turn Away'. Beneath, a plaque had been affixed – words engraved deep in the steel, no longer gleaming, a message from Mutolo's grandfather proclaiming the ruin a dangerous place and commanding travellers and treasure-hunters who valued their lives to 'walk no farther'.

"Really makes you feel good, doesn't it?" Udoc said as he squinted at the sign.

Rokura dismounted, patting Arrow's neck. "You need not travel any further. This is not a recovery; we will merely confirm the rebels passed this way. Cosequ?"

"Rokura has the right of it. Prime Scout, report back to Lieutenant Kini. Mobilise but hold for my call."

"Yes, Commander."

"Hmmm. Is this a mistake?" Rokura asked once the others had left.

"Going alone? No, it'll be exactly like the time we chased the panther into that forest fire."

"That could have ended better."

Cosequ rubbed at his unshaven cheek. "We don't need to travel far to confirm what we suspect."

"Or at all." He lifted the disc with its faint purple glow. "See?"

"What if they left someone behind? Injured or unwell. We could get valuable information, whether they be friend or foe."

"Very well. After which, we'll return to the post and send word to the king. I need to plan my next move," Rokura replied, a touch of hesitation holding his feet in place. Whatever the king ordered, whatever the truth of the prisoners' identity, the people of the villages deserved rescue. And at the very least, for someone to make an attempt. After all, what value could the land of Nasaru claim if no-one would seek out even the poorest of citizens?

Cosequ's suggestion, however slim a likelihood, had to be investigated. And yet, the reputation of the melting city spread far beyond the borders of the lost nation of the False Ones.

"A fine plan. And it's not like we're close enough to catch them, anyway, based on your estimations. They're already beneath the mountain or dead by now."

"Most likely."

Cosequ started up the stair, drawing his blade as he did, checking on the Coral bracelet he wore upon his opposite wrist. "We can't wait all day."

"Right." Rokura drew a throwing dagger and strode after his cousin. "Have you actually entered the city before?"

"No. I climbed the stair once, not long after my posting, but didn't go in."

"Are the stories true?"

"In a way. I won't spoil it for you."

On they strode. The stair was leading to a plateau, both the walls and shadows growing. It was not long enough to weary his legs, nor so steep as to stop trade, especially with a landing halfway up, but holding the high ground would have been useful in repelling attackers.

At the top, thoughts of military advantage vanished.

Vi Mekadymu.

The melting city was a forest of dark, stone trunks – or better, *pillars* of regular size and width, all arranged in erratic patterns. The broadest were like towers but most were smaller, closer to mighty trees, and many were thinner still.

Not a single one seemed fragile enough to topple.

And yet the pillars led to nothing.

Supported nothing.

Concealed very little too, as where they rose from the patterned stone floor, the rest of the mountain was visible beyond. The paved floor stretched on, littered with stone, rocks and even more yellowed weeds, some twisted into grey. At times, the ground was uneven and cracked, places where water might well have collected.

Despite the dry day, a sense that rain poured upon the ruin could not be denied – for the surface of the pillars gleamed bright, as though rainwater streamed down from an unseen storm.

"It is quite the sight during a sunset," Cosequ said, speaking softly.

"You've seen it?"

He nodded. "And that's about all. Couldn't go in very far back then... felt like I was being watched. It became too much, somehow." He lifted his bracelet. "I couldn't even use this to strengthen myself. And even if I had, there was just nothing to strike anyway. The *feeling* drove me out, not an enemy I could see. But that was years and years ago; I'm stronger now."

The ruin seemed powerfully empty still, with no sense of anyone watching. No traces even of the passage of the prisoners ahead.

"What's farther in?" Rokura asked. "I recall little about the stories."

"Supposedly, an amphitheatre where the False Ones conducted their rituals and experiments, and that's all – just more of the columns. Some of the legends claim they once supported buildings, but I doubt we'll ever find out," Cosequ replied. "We just have to find those prisoners or their trail, right?"

"Right."

## CHAPTER 29. – MEI

The lid upon Rinbe's casket of stone did not slide open.

Anyo frowned, then gripped the casket harder, leaning in to strain against the tomb. Yet it did not move, not even after he waved Hanibalo and Katonga closer to help and together they fought it, veins and muscles in their necks bulging.

Eventually, Anyo fell back with a muttered curse. "It is beyond us."

Hanibalo straightened, folding his arms. "I believe I know your answer, lad, but what say you to trying to break it open?"

Anyo was shaking his head before Hanibalo finished speaking, gesturing to a symbol carved into the stone. "Even if we had enough Coral to break the seal, not in a thousand years would we do that."

Mei glanced between them but there was no bitter feud about to erupt; the older man only nodded and Anyo continued to stare at Rinbe's tomb. When he started to circle it, examining the surface without issuing any further orders, Katonga offered to forage for firewood. "We can camp inside the building, right?"

Anyo murmured his assent without looking up.

Mei hesitated to offer any further help. It didn't seem

likely she could blast the tomb apart, though it might have been possible to crack it at least, but Anyo would hardly allow any attempt.

And more, did she actually *want* to help her captors?

Finally, Anyo stood with a sigh. "Let us take a meal and consider our choices."

"Still plenty of unanswered questions too," Hanibalo added. "We don't know what is or isn't in there."

For Mei, the question of Marhyn was of most concern.

"I'll find some wood for a fire," Katonga said as he started back along the passage.

Mei followed the others, her question remaining unanswered when they climbed free. More, Mei found herself hesitating at the kitchen, as a sense of cold and *illness* washed over her, flowing from the building's entryway. "Something is wrong."

Anyo and Hanibalo had drawn their swords, tension clear in their movements as they spread into the room...

*There.*

Some *thing* stood over the prone form of Katonga.

Squat, dark, and green, it was still head and shoulders taller than Anyo, its bulk seeming to fill the room beyond its actual size. The sense of illness poured from the creature, and though it stood upright on two heavily muscled legs, its limbs were webbed and spiked – it was no man or woman.

The monster was more toad-like, with a distended stomach that glistened with slime, and a broad, bony-looking jaw. Its mouth was large enough to crush a head with a single bite, and when it turned to hiss at them, slime oozed over a row of ridges unlike teeth.

"Back, fiend!" Anyo cried, waving his blade.

Milky green eyes did not seem at all afraid. The mighty toad-creature simply stepped away from Katonga and flung its arms up in a flash. Anyo's sword twitched and something struck the stone wall, bouncing to roll across the floor.

A slime-covered prong, its tip sharp as any knife.

Mei shrank back into the hallway, caught between confusion and fear. Had the monster's other hand swept up something from the floor during its attack? When the thing raised a hand to its wide mouth and began to chew, Mei had her answer – as despite the way it seemed to be focused on its eating, its orb-like eyes were wide-spaced enough that the creature was well aware of both Anyo and Hanibalo.

Whatever it held, whatever it was gnawing on, it was going to use.

"We will draw its attention, Mei," Anyo said without turning. "Take your chance."

And then the two leapt for the monster from opposite sides.

Before Mei could respond, the creature spat a great ball of green and black murk at Anyo. At the same time, it flung another prong at Hanibalo. The prong lodged into Hanibalo's arm and he stumbled to the ground, limbs seemingly frozen already.

Despite the gunk that covered Anyo, he had not broken his charge. He thrust his blade into the monster's stomach with a cry of fury. The sword did not penetrate far, but it was enough to bring bright green blood and drive the toad back toward the door.

Yet Anyo collapsed, just as frozen as the others.

The thing did not flee. It stepped toward her, great bulk gleaming and the stench of infection and poison growing.

Mei blasted the toad-monster with a psychic blow, stunning the creature.

She struck again.

It reeled back this time and so Mei gathered as much strength as she could and hurled her power forth – not aiming for its mind this time, but for the body. The invisible blow sent the creature tumbling outside where it crashed to the earth.

There, it lay still a moment.

Mei wobbled on her feet, reaching for a wall. But she did not let her gaze leave the monster until it moved – and it began to crawl away! It was making only slow progress as it crossed the vale's floor, but it was leaving. *Thank the Guardians.* The thing was heading back to the marsh, hopefully. Probably to a nest somewhere within.

Had it followed them all the way to Rinbe's abandoned home?

She frowned after the toad-creature. *I don't think it's coming back soon, at least.*

Mei slumped against the wall to catch her breath. "This is my chance."

Nothing stood in her way now; Anyo and his men were no threat. Mei pushed herself up and approached them. Anyo was unconscious, his face and chest covered in the muck, his breathing fast and uneven.

Hanibalo was equally incapacitated, though his entire body had stiffened in a paralysis from the prong. His eyes were wide open and he too was breathing. Katonga appeared the same, a prong in his torso.

None would survive if the thing returned.

Or if Marhyn appeared – assuming the toad-monster had

not devoured the sorcerer? It was possible but was it likely?

Even leaving her captors to recover on their own could result in their deaths *without* the arrival of traitors or monsters... for who knew how strong the poison?

Mei found herself unable to take another step.

Did the men before her really deserve death? The Nasaru were no friends. *Not my responsibility either.* But the memory of Master Arun's voice echoed in her mind, about a healer's duty to preserve life. She carried enough herbs to save them, or at least, to make a good attempt.

Yet didn't Iggy come first? *He* needed her more. And now was her best and probably only chance to escape.

Mei folded her arms.

# CHAPTER 30. – ROKURA

Barely a few strides into the ruin, Rokura paused to rest a palm against one of the columns. Bone dry. Somewhere beneath the surface, it seemed something flowed. Faint, but if he closed his eyes, the sense of movement, of latent power grew stronger...

"Do you feel that?" Cosequ asked. "We're being watched, just like the last time I was here."

Rokura opened his eyes.

His cousin stood with an empty Coral vial in hand, eyes glittering black as he stared between the columns. The magic would aid Cosequ's sight *and* perception, but would it be enough to pierce whatever veil the False Ones had set up?

"Where?" Rokura turned in a careful circle. The sense of being observed was entirely absent – the ruins were just as empty as before.

"Everywhere. That's the problem."

But no faces appeared from between the columns, nothing rose from the dust-covered stone nor loomed in the blue sky above. The ruin was empty... on the surface, at least.

He kept his blades ready, nevertheless.

"It's as though the whole place..."

Cosequ was still talking, but his voice was fading and darkness was smothering the sun – so swift that Rokura flinched.

And then he found himself in a shimmering field of flowers spread beneath a midnight-blue sky. And while the stars shone overhead, light also responded from below, gossamer lines of gold that climbed up to meet the stars from all around.

He reached out to touch one but his fingers found naught but air, though the light glowed through his very flesh.

Was this place the mysterious part of the Vi Mekadymu that drove people mad?

*It's a place of tranquil beauty.*

"Cousin?" Rokura turned, calling again, but Cosequ was nowhere to be seen.

How to escape?

Simply walk on and hope to come across a building? An exit of some sort? Anything save for the endless rows of golden tulips and lilies.

Yet he had barely taken a dozen steps when his foot snagged.

Rokura crashed to his knees in a cloud of pollen. It stung his eyes but tasted of sweet fruit. Growling, he rose to rub at his eyes until the pain eased. Had he already fallen prey to Vi Mekadymu?

The pollen was going to have some irreversible effect, surely?

He could not move.

Or at least, his legs had been bound by the delicate tendrils of grey and purple, with more golden petals spilling forth in glimmering clouds of bright pollen. Not a single plant in the field ought to have contained the strength to hold him in place, but he could only move his torso, arms and head.

And when the tendrils climbed to his knees, leaving golden streaks upon his clothing, they stopped. A pleasant warmth joined the sweet scent in the air, soothing but hardly enough to lull him into giving up.

He drew a dagger and slashed at the flowers.

Screams erupted.

Agony forced its way into his body, surging in through his eyes and nose – even his ears as blood filled his mouth. The pain wracked his body then, creeping down his throat toward his chest. And he was powerless to stop it.

His muscles constricted, tighter and tighter…

Clear white light blazed.

It seared enough that tears flowed down his cheeks, even as he raised a hand to shield his eyes. But as much as the whiteness burned, it cleansed too.

*You can open your eyes now.*

Calm spread through his heaving chest, his limbs and his mind; pain easing in his face as flickering images of a darkened, glowing field of flowers vanished to be replaced by the ruins of Vi Mekadymu.

Beneath a sunny sky, the columns were still 'melting'. And sitting next to him, his featureless face half-hidden by Rokura's old, hooded cloak, was the runaway from Nokema.

Iggy.

The source of the light?

"How did... You came to save me?" Rokura asked.

The young man nodded. *I owed you. After all, you saved me first. Consider me saving your cousin part of my debt, also.*

"Then you have my deep appreciation," he said, glancing to the prone form of Cosequ, who breathed easy but was not yet awake.

Iggy shrugged.

"I am serious, Iggy. A life is a precious gift and I have good to do yet in this world. I would not care to lose a chance to complete that duty."

*Well, you were the first outside my home to offer me help.* He paused. *I want to believe that I am not so bitter that your actions meant so little to me that I couldn't answer your call.*

"My call?" Rokura rose to a sitting position, noting that his clothing was no longer covered in golden pollen.

*Just a cry of desperation, but I think this place made your call strong enough to reach me.*

"And you knew it was me?"

*Easily.*

"I see." Though he did not understand the specifics, why not? It made as much sense as anything else about the ruin.

Or the young lad, for that matter.

*But I can't protect you from this place all day – there is an immense power farther within,* Iggy added as he stood. *It's probably safest to leave.*

"We must reach the south," Rokura said, glancing to the looming mountain. "They passed through this place."

*Then they know more than either of us.*

Rokura pushed himself up to join the lad with a nod. A troubling truth indeed. What or who exactly *did* the rebels have to protect them? And if even someone like the mysterious young man beside him could not guarantee passage through the ruin and mountain, then that left the highway.

Eroya's wooden disc would still lead to Brutan and whatever

nest he might have built for his nefarious goals... in time.

But what cost would such a delay reap?

*I would travel with you, for a time.*

He glanced down at the lad. "You would?"

*Yes. There is someone in the south that I am seeking,* Iggy said. *Supposedly, she can help me.*

Rokura hesitated, and a stab of shame followed. Refusing the one who had just saved his life was poor form of the highest order... yet he would not travel with the skull the lad had chosen to carry around.

Iggy opened his cloak, revealing naught but the other clothes Rokura had given the lad. *The skull is somewhere safe, but I can still speak to her.*

Once again, having his thoughts read, or at least his concerns anticipated brought little comfort. But he nodded. "Then welcome, Iggy. I do not know where the rebels' trail will lead me exactly."

*I do not know exactly where I go either. It is hard to be certain. Just that I must pass through the town of Atanoph.*

Atanoph. A somewhat unsavoury place. "If the rebels hide within the far side of these mountains, we will pass Atanoph near enough," he said. "Though it is not a kind city. There are few who would seem likely to help you."

*I am not certain of that.*

"Who do you seek there?"

*A location for the Mistress of Obsidian.*

He straightened. Another dark legend, not someone who could be trifled with – if she still existed. "Iggy. If she has survived the decades, she is said to be *very* dangerous. A sorcerer of shadow, if human at all. And that is only if you could find her to begin with."

*Even so, there is no-one else who can give me a face, Rokura.*

# ACKNOWLEDGMENTS

To each and everyone who supported this trilogy on Kickstarter, thank you so much, these books are for you.

It's been a long wait - but without everyone below, the wait would have gone on and on and there would have been absolutely *zero chance* that all three books would have been released together, so thank you again!

**Heiko Koenig ~ Vitor Publishing ~ Jeff Lewis ~ Daryl Parat ~ Jesper Pettersen ~ Larry Couch ~ Supreme Emperor Ben Mariner ~ The Creative Fund by BackerKit ~ Stephen Ballentine ~ Esapekka Eriksson ~ John Idlor ~ David Lars Chamberlain ~ Robin Hill ~ Virginia McClain ~ Señor Neo ~ John Mackie ~ Jason Cordero ~ Richard Bunting ~ Debbie Phillips ~ Jason ~ L.M. Lacee ~ William C. Tracy ~ Erin Himrod ~ C.Wilson ~ Sven Lugar ~ Ian Linford ~ Monica Elida Forssell ~ Astridd ~ Technewszone.com**

~ Samantha Landstrom ~ Anne Walker ~ Cheryl Linford ~ Zac ~ Shirley S ~ Richard Novak ~ nny ~ Aramanth Dawe ~ Thomas Polk ~ Maddalena Tarallo ~ Donna ~ Mitchell S. ~ Trava Buono ~ Lee Dunning ~ Levid José de Jesús Montes Sánchez ~ Peter & Andy ~ Fritha Blackwood ~ Leo Collis ~ Jamie-Lee Graafmans ~ Michaela Miles ~ Belinda Mellor ~ Katherine Shipman ~ Patty Jansen ~ Jessica Ward ~ Jazmine Baldwin ~ C. Gockel ~ Sven Grams ~ Matthian ~ Scott Freisthler ~ Rhianne R. ~ Blade ~ Emma Adams ~ C.Niehot ~ Becky James ~ sabrinaweb71 ~ Tony and Ben Muzi ~ Joe Monson ~ Tao Wong ~ Zee ~ Ellen Pilcher ~ Jesper Pettersen ~ Award-Winning Author Wendy Scott.

I am also once again in debt to Brooke! And to Rebekah at Vivid Covers for the amazing set of covers that not only showcase the main cast, but strike the perfect mood.

I must also thank Amanda at Phoenix Editing for always going beyond what I ask (especially with Volume 3!) and also David at David Schembri Studios for the formatting – I know I gave him some extra work with the range of fonts!

Ashley Capes

## A NOTE FROM ASHLEY

Hello! I hope you enjoyed *A Drifting Sun* and thank you for reading.

If you could help me out by leaving an honest review of the book at your place of purchase, that would be fantastic! Long or short, bad or good, it all helps.

**As all three volumes of the Exiles Trilogy were released together, you can already sample or purchase *Exiles: Volume 2 (The Faceless Moon)* at your retailer of choice!**

AND if you'd like to sign up to my newsletter (https://www.subscribepage.com/b5w1k0) you'll be the first to know when future Exiles books are released. You'll also have first access to preview chapters and pre-release editions of my other stories, in addition to being automatically added into the draw for giveaways.

Ashley

www.ingramcontent.com/pod-product-compliance
Lightning Source LLC
Chambersburg PA
CBHW020513120726
47904CB00003B/813